M000021429

# MELANIE LEAVEY

# Wind Singer

*Book Two of the Sea Glass Trilogy*

Wishing you all of the
magic!

Melanie Leavey

**THREE RAVENS**
**P R E S S**

*First published by Three Ravens Press 2020*

*Copyright © 2020 by Melanie Leavey*

*All rights reserved. No part of this publication may be reproduced, stored or transmitted in any form or by any means, electronic, mechanical, photocopying, recording, scanning, or otherwise without written permission from the publisher. It is illegal to copy this book, post it to a website, or distribute it by any other means without permission.*

*This novel is entirely a work of fiction. The names, characters and incidents portrayed in it are the work of the author's imagination. Any resemblance to actual persons, living or dead, events or localities is entirely coincidental.*

*Melanie Leavey asserts the moral right to be identified as the author of this work.*

*Designations used by companies to distinguish their products are often claimed as trademarks. All brand names and product names used in this book and on its cover are trade names, service marks, trademarks and registered trademarks of their respective owners. The publishers and the book are not associated with any product or vendor mentioned in this book. None of the companies referenced within the book have endorsed the book.*

*Second edition*

*ISBN: 978-1-7771431-3-8*

*This book was professionally typeset on Reedsy.*
*Find out more at reedsy.com*

*for Savannah,*
*who stood at the edge of everything and chose to stay*

# Contents

# Acknowledgement

Producing a second book is a bit like producing a second child; everyone is pleased but there's nowhere near the same amount of fuss, despite the fact it often feels a far more daunting venture.

So many thanks to those who have, and continue to, prop me up. Your words of encouragement, your genuine delight in *Skelly* and photos of your copies "in the wild" have done more to bolster my flagging nerves than you could ever possibly know.

Special thanks to Susan Rizzo, for reminding why I'm doing this strange, mad thing...

...and to my husband, Brandt, for always believing I can pull it off.

# Prologue

He didn't know how long he'd been drifting. The push and pull of the tide was gentle now, rocking him, lulling him into a state of half-awareness like a mother rocks her infant to sleep. The violent storm had subsided - how long ago? - his concept of time was skewed. Once, he'd measured his days in limitlessness. But that was before.

The sun dappled through the surface of the sea; he could see it glowing with a suffused light - a vague orange blur above the grey-green of the upper levels of the ocean, drawing him higher, out of the depths of his home.

He squeezed his eyes shut, willing it to be untrue. But the weight of his limbs and the sting of salt on his skin whispered his denial.

*You will remember*

That was his last memory before the storm. The ring of faces surrounding him, sharp-featured, gills and fronds fluttering in the deep current. They circled him; accusing, mocking, begging to tear him to pieces, if only she'd give the word.

1

The price of pride, she'd said. Such arrogance! How dare he presume to allow it? The very thing that was forbidden. How dare he presume to risk the very existence of their people? How dare he allow, no, encourage, the taint of the land upon those born to the sea?

He'd tried to plead with her. He had, after all, held the wind for them. Wasn't that enough to show he'd meant only well? How could he be held responsible for the treachery of the land-walkers?

His people.

He felt the beginning of something deep in his chest, an unfamiliar ache. His people were gone from him now, scattered across all of the seas - some of them beyond the reaches of the tides. It had been their choice, of course, made willingly, but at what price? So many of them, eager for the adventure, curious of what lay beyond the boundaries of water. He'd tried to tell them, tried to warn them of the cost, but they hadn't listened.

She'd made him watch. Their screams tore into him, shredding what was left of his soul as they'd changed - exchanging one life for another. An eternal punishment for turning their backs on their ocean home. They were bound in their own way, he had thought, after, as the glittering shards of what they'd once been settled into the sand at his feet. Not quite of the sea and not quite of the land, they hung somewhere between the two, always torn. A bitter irony, that.

*You are banished. You will walk the earth for a thousand thousand years. You will hold the betrayal of your people as a weight around you - with every step of your earthbound feet. You will never again know the caress of your home upon your skin. You will never again dive the depths of what was once your kingdom.*

*But you **will** remember.*

2

The change itself had nearly killed him. He wished it had; he would have happily surrendered to oblivion. But she'd kept him alive. That was the point of the punishment, after all. Death would have been easy.

He knew he was getting higher. Any minute and he'd break the surface. He could sense the brightness of the sun and the shift in temperature of the water.

*Will I ever come back?* he'd asked, when it was over and he lay, broken, at her feet.

She hadn't answered, only placed a hand on his shoulder and lifted him to stand.

Then she'd raised the storm that cast them all away — the taint of land would not be tolerated. Walking amongst mortals wasn't an option in their watery kingdom the way it was among other realms. It had been a mercy, the storm that scattered them. It meant a chance, at least. The only one she had to offer. But it was something.

Briefly, he'd struggled. He'd tried to swim down, to fight the compulsion to rise. But the storm had purpose and he knew it was pointless to resist. They had all gone. He was alone in the churning sea that no longer felt like his skin but was alien and harsh. He felt the beginnings of loss, the sting of salt and the strange pressure in his lungs. He'd been to the surface, of course, many times, but always by choice and always as part of the sea, rather than a foreign object that was to be purged.

At last it came; the searing agony of the first breath of air. It tore through him like a knife, piercing every blood cell with its strangeness. Shuddering, he gasped. Too much. Not enough. He couldn't regulate it.

Ah then, he thought, through a haze of pain. This is how it will end. Well, enough. He was happy to go and so faded into

3

the blackness.

\* \* \*

"Well, then pet," said Morag, smiling down at the bobbing mop of red curls, "What've you got to tell me today?"

"Nothing much, Gran, I'm sorry to say. It's a terrible shortage of magic we're having."

Cliona stood with her hands on her hips, her face creased into a frown as she looked down at the collection of pebbles and sticks piled at her yellow-wellied feet.

"Aye, well. 'Tis bound to happen from time to time you see? If the world keeps galloping off like it does, soon there won't be but a single wish in the sea!"

Morag sighed and straightened, wincing at the protests of her creaking joints. She reached out a crooked-fingered hand to her five-year-old granddaughter.

"Right, let's have a look, will we? Every bit helps, you know. Even the smallest bit of the sea magic…"

"Will help to keep the selkie people safe!" chimed in the little girl, repeating the story she'd been told since she was but a baby in her grandmother's arms.

Morag smiled, her eyes sparkling at the gap-toothed grin of the little girl.

"That's right, my darling. That's right."

# Chapter 1

Cliona buried herself deeper under the bedclothes. The wind rattling the windowpanes and the sound of rain splattering onto the glass and drumming on the roof above her did nothing to entice her to leave the warm nest.

"Cliona!"

Her brother's voice echoed, for the third time, up the long, narrow staircase.

"Get your lazy arse out of bed, I've got nets that need mending!"

Cliona grinned. Their mother would now be scolding Ewan for his language. Thirty-two years as a fisherman's wife but she wouldn't tolerate foul language under her roof. Both her da and Ewan took every opportunity to taunt her with that rule and while well she knew they were doing it and went along with great good humour, she still lost no opportunity to berate them for it.

The sound of booted feet tramping up the wooden stairs only made Cliona burrow more deeply. The last thing she wanted on a day like today was to go down to the quayside and spend it mending nets. The fact that she'd already agreed to do it only produced a slight niggling guilt.

Ewan hammered on the door.

"Come on, you feckless creature," he said. "It's practically dinner time and you're still lounging around like lady of the manor."

"Go away," came the muffled reply. "It's miserable out there. Can't you do it yourself?"

"Yes, obviously. But you're faster and your knots are better. Must be your advanced training and delicate girlish fingers."

"Flattery will get you nowhere," she replied, smiling despite herself.

"I've got tea," wheedled Ewan. "And a bacon roll."

Now that, thought Cliona, was the sort of bribery she could get behind.

She groaned, throwing back the warm eiderdown and sitting up.

"You may enter," she said, her tone mockingly imperious.

The latch lifted and Ewan came in, balancing a napkin-wrapped bundle in the crook of his elbow as he opened the door with the other hand.

"Now you really are like the lady of the manor," he said, handing her the steaming mug of tea which she took gratefully, cupping her hands around its warmth.

There was no central heating in the tall stone house and by morning, the heat of the fires that rose from the first floor had long dissipated. Whoever was awake first had the task of kindling the kitchen fire, but it took several hours to reach the attic floor where Cliona had her little room. A couple of years ago, when Cliona had complained about it, her da had made it very clear that every decent hard-working person was up and working before it got cold so if she *was* cold, she'd clearly been in bed too long. The sulky seventeen-year-old Cliona had simply asked her gran to help her make a quilted eiderdown.

"Alright then?" asked Ewan, sitting himself on the edge of her bed. His face was furrowed in a worried frown, but he was doing his best not to appear so. He knew from experience that his sister did not take kindly to fussing and concern.

Cliona took a sip of tea then a bite of bacon roll. She closed her eyes in an expression of sheer bliss. Her mam was a genius with the homemade baps.

Eventually, after she savoured, chewed and swallowed, she shrugged.

"It's still happening, if that's what you mean," she said, with an air of nonchalance.

"Are they bad?"

Ewan's dark eyes bore into hers. Cliona wished he didn't know about the headaches that had been plaguing her of late, but he'd found her, late one morning, sitting in the corner of the boatshed, hands clenched over her face, moaning.

She shrugged again, trying not to make eye contact.

She loved Ewan with all her heart. Almost ten years her senior, he'd been her hero her whole life. Besides Gran, he was the only member of her family who seemed to understand what it was to be her. He couldn't relate, of course, because he was fully immersed in island life and the minute he'd finished school, he was out on the boat, full-time with their da. He would have gone sooner if their mam hadn't insisted that he finish school first. It was one of many arguments that had raged around the table at mealtimes in Cliona's early years. So, he although he couldn't fathom what it was to want so desperately to leave Glencarragh, he'd taken her side when she'd insisted she was going away to university and had even visited her a couple of times in Glasgow.

"About the same, "she lied. "I'm sure they'll pass. Gran gave me one of her potions and it seems to help."

More lies, she thought, sighing inwardly. The biggest lie of all being that what she was experiencing weren't exactly just headaches, but she couldn't very well tell anyone the whole truth. She'd be carted off to the loony bin in no time.

Ewan ran a hand through his thick, black hair. He was 'classical Glencarragh', as Cliona often teased him. Black eyes, black hair, startling good looks. She insisted that the beautiful people were the real reason the tourists came in droves and not the story that the seals in the bay were actually selkies. Cliona, on the other hand, stood out like a sore thumb. Green eyes and bright red hair. The smattering of freckles across her cheeks and bridge of her nose only added to her otherness, everyone else on Glencarragh seemingly of the pure porcelain complexion variety.

"It's no wonder I don't fit in," she'd once complained to her best friend, Iain who was also 'classical Glencarragh'. "I even *look* different from you lot."

"Well isn't that a relief, though?" he'd replied. "All of us looking the same is a bit boring. And besides, we don't all look the same. Think of Alys MacFinlay."

Cliona had giggled. That poor unfortunate was blonde and, at the time, a victim of a severe case of adolescent acne.

"Besides, it's only to be expected," he'd added, seeing her mood lift, "you being a changeling and everything."

That was another joke between them. He'd once told her, when they were still small, that *his* mam had told him that the faeries must have left her on the doorstep because no-one, not even Cliona's own parents, ever thought there'd be another baby in the Stewart family.

"It's alright, Ewan," said Cliona, kicking her brother gently from under the covers. "Don't be such an old woman. Besides, you've got enough to worry about with this weather."

Ewan gave her a brief smile then switched his attention to the window. It was streaked with rain and the wind continued to find ways in through the old casement, making the curtains tremble.

"Aye, that's true," he agreed.

"Will Da still expect you to keep going out?"

Ewan snorted. He and their father often had disagreements over suitable fishing weather, among other things.

"More than likely," he said, rubbing his hands down the thighs of his thick corduroy trousers. "The old bugger doesn't like to miss too many dances."

Cliona nodded. Fishing wasn't the lucrative venture it had once been in the waters around Glencarragh. Despite years of strict and careful fishing practices, there simply weren't the hauls of years gone by. There were plenty of theories, some logical, other more prone to flights of fantasy. A current favourite among the more superstitious folk was that it was the old legend of a vengeful faery queen of the sea, coming again to exact her punishment on the people of Glencarragh. According to the folklore, she'd been cheated by some far distant generations of inhabitants and had loathed the island ever since. The more pragmatic minds felt it was because of the new pelagic trawlers that could go further and bring in larger hauls, leaving little for the small, traditional fishing families.

"Did you mention to him again about the offer for doing the tours?"

Ewan winced, reaching up to scratch his unruly beard. There were a few grey hairs in it, noticed Cliona. Too soon for that. He was only just thirty-four on his last birthday.

"Aye, I did."

"And," prodded Cliona. "It's the perfect solution, Ewan. He's got to see sense. If you went out on the tour boats, you wouldn't have to do the winter fishing. You'd make more money and it's much…."

Her voice trailed off, not wanting to resurrect that argument again.

"Safer? That's what you were going to say, isn't it?"

Ewan gave her a hard look. When he looked at her like that, she could see their father in him. In manner, if not in temperament.

Cliona returned his stare; unlike her father, she wasn't intimidated by her older brother.

"Yes, if you must know. But I wasn't going to carry on because I really don't want us to be fighting, Ewan. You know how I feel about winter fishing. And Gran backs me up on that so you can't accuse me of womanly hysteria."

"No, lass. That's Da's job," grinned Ewan, his mood shifting again.

Cliona rolled her eyes.

"Now get lost," she said, flinging back the bedclothes and wincing at the sudden blast of cold air against her bare legs. She tucked her knees up under her nightgown. "If you want me to come and mend your sodding nets, I need to get myself sorted."

"Aye, go on then. Try not to be an age," said her brother, reaching over to tussle her hair, something he knew she hated.

She swatted at him and he rose, laughing, towards the door.

When he was gone, she allowed her face to fall and her shoulders to sag. Closing her eyes, she rested her forehead on her raised knees.

10

Please, let it stop, she whispered. Let it stop.

But she knew it wouldn't. It would no more stop than the tide.

Sighing, she forced herself out of bed and got dressed, shivering in the cold air of her little bedroom. The wind hurled rain against the windowpanes, as she tugged on thick woolen tights, reminding her of exactly how much she hated everything about living on Glencarragh.

Well, she acknowledged, not everything. She had Iain, her best friend since the first day of nursery school and she had her family. Even her mercurial father, whose moods shifted like the weather for which Glencarragh was notorious. And Gran, always Gran.

*That's it, then*, she thought, shoving aside her grumbling thoughts of escaping back to the mainland. She laced up the heavy boots she always wore when she worked down at the quayside. *I'm stuck here. Bound by the sheer enormity of love I have for the people in my life. Why else would I come back here, instead of staying in Glasgow when I finished my degree?* She had no answer for that, only that she'd found herself standing on the crowded platform at Hillhead one grey, dismal morning, missing her family with a deep, insistent ache. It seemed that once the flurry and excitement of university was over, there was little to hold her to the noisy streets of the city. On her worst days, she considered it a personal failing. On better days, it filled her with a sort of expansive warmth that emanated from somewhere deep in her chest and she couldn't imagine ever leaving the stormy, wind-ravaged crag of an island upon which she'd had the great misfortune to be born. Still, she'd hedged her bets and was waiting to hear from a prestigious design house in Paris who, for the first time in almost a decade, were taking on an international intern. She'd figure out what happened next if she was accepted, her chances of which, if she were honest with herself, were probably quite slim. Her collection of awards, letters of recommendation and incredible success in Glasgow would mean little against the graduates of some of the biggest fashion schools in the world.

She glanced back at her bedroom cum studio. The white plaster walls were covered with posters she'd begged from the travel agent on the mainland. The bright colours and exotic destinations had carried her through the long winter nights of her teens when it seemed like her world would never see sunlight again. She'd had it all planned. A fat notebook, bulging with thick, creamy paper still sat, well-thumbed, on her bedside table. It was stuffed with maps and lists and vision boards and a rough outline of what she dreamed of doing. First, a degree in fashion design, followed by a prestigious internship, her wild success with which she would have her pick of opportunities, all of which would involve world travel.

Another blast of rain jolted her from her daydream.

One day, she promised herself as she clattered down the stairs into the kitchen. Maybe one day the wind will blow hard enough to carry me away from here.

\* \* \*

"What time is this, then?"

In response, Cliona glanced pointedly at the kitchen clock. She gestured with her mug, which she'd refilled from the big Brown Betty on the kitchen table.

"Looks to me like almost nine," she replied, "At least, that's what the clock says."

12

"Cliona," warned her mother. Helen Stewart stood, kneading dough at the far side of the room. "Don't start, the pair of you."

"I'm not starting anything," said Cliona, leaning against the Welsh dresser as she sipped her tea. "I was asked a silly question and answered accordingly."

Her mother sighed, blowing a strand of hair that had escaped her efforts to restrain it into a bun. Her hair, at least, Cliona shared with her mother. The colour was different, but the unruly curls were the one thing that assured her that she wasn't actually a changeling after all.

"It's a bloody sin, that's what it is," retorted her father. "Your brother has been waiting on you for hours. A whole days' work could be done by now, and here's you, swanning down the stairs at this hour like Lady Whatnot. You're not in Glasgow now, my girl. It's time you buckled down and started acting like a member of this family, now that you've got that nonsense out of your system."

Cliona bit back her reply, catching another warning glance from her mother.

"Cliona pet," she said, nodding towards her daughter with a questioning eye, taking in the Liberty print pinafore that she'd repurposed from a set of curtains she'd found in a Glasgow thrift shop. She wore a lime green cardigan - the pattern of her own design - over it and striped woolen tights. "Are you sure that's a suitable costume for being down at the boat shed? It's teeming down out there."

"I hadn't noticed," replied Cliona, dryly, pouring the dregs of her tea into the gleaming Belfast sink. The rain streamed down the window. Cliona stared out of it, unseeing, as she stood rinsing her mug.

"And yes, it's entirely suitable because it's what *I* want to wear. I have very little control over my life these days, mam, as well you know," she flicked her eyes towards her father, but he'd gone back to his newspaper. "Therefore, my choice of clothing is my way to wrest some semblance of autonomy into my days."

A grunt emanated from behind the newspaper.

Her mother smiled a weary smile.

"Alright, pet. As you like. I just wouldn't want all your hard work getting spoiled by engine grease or…"

"The stink of fish?" finished Cliona, unable to help herself. "Well I'd say that's fairly much permeated my whole being at this point, wouldn't you?"

The look that crossed her mother's face made her immediately regretful.

*Mouth,* she admonished herself. *Just shut your ratty mouth.*

"It's alright, mam," she said, her tone softening. "I have an old filleting apron of Grandad's that I wear when I'm doing the nets. I'll be careful."

Her mother nodded, wordlessly and returned to the bread dough.

Cliona reached for the tea towel to dry her mug when it hit her.

*Oh no,* she groaned inwardly. *Not again. Not now.*

A wave of dizziness and nausea was followed by a stabbing pain that sliced from the back of her head to behind her eyes. A low buzzing sound, like a bad telephone connection started from somewhere deep in her brain and the faint sound of someone speaking crackled through. She put out a hand to steady herself. The mug slipped through nerveless fingers and crashed to the slate floor before she crumpled into a heap beside the sink.

14

# Chapter 2

When she opened her eyes, she was staring at the ceiling in the sitting room. Anxious faces appeared in her line of vision.

"She's awake," breathed Helen, who was clutching Cliona's hand between her own. "Thank you, blessed Mother," she muttered, closing her own eyes briefly.

"How are you feeling, pet?"

Gran appeared beside Helen; her lined face furrowed even more deeply.

"Careful now, don't sit up too quickly," she warned, reached out a gentle hand to steady her granddaughter as Cliona shifted gingerly into a sitting position.

"There, that's better. Here, drink this, it'll ease your head."

Morag handed her a steaming mug of something that smelt like unwashed woolen socks. Feverfew, probably with a bit of willow bark and some chamomile and peppermint to try and hide the taste, recited Cliona automatically in her head. Plus, whatever Gran's secret ingredient was. *Not enough peppermint,* she added to herself, grimacing as she sipped the familiar brew. If it wasn't because it worked, she wouldn't have entertained it again after the very first sip she'd taken. No amount of honey could mask the foul taste. But it worked, so she continued to

15

drink.

"How did I get here?" she asked.

Her mother and grandmother exchanged worried looks.

"I mean, to the sitting room," said Cliona, rolling her eyes affectionately at the two women. "I seem to remember I was in the kitchen when the voice…when I last heard you speaking."

Another exchange of looks, only this time, her gran looked away.

Her mam cleared her throat.

"Your da carried you in," she said. "We had to get you off the cold floor. He's gone to get more coal for the fire."

She gestured towards the hearth where the fire crackled merrily.

"A fire in here?" said Cliona. "At this hour of the day? Have we won the pools or something?"

Morag chuckled.

"Well, you're obviously feeling better," she said, with some relief. "You've got your ratty mouth back."

"It's your da's doing," said her mother, her voice soft with quiet warning. "He was worried when you fainted like that. Please don't make a fuss."

Cliona pressed her lips together and nodded.

Just then, her da returned with a full coal scuttle. When he saw her sitting up, relief flashed across his surly features before they settled back into their customary scowl. He nodded.

"You're up, then" he said, shoveling more coal onto the fire. "Alright?"

"Yes, thanks, Da," she said. "You needn't bother with the fire…"

"Never mind, that," he said, his voice gruff. "You'll need to sit for a minute and this room is cold. The wind creeps in, as

16

you know. I'll go down to the quayside and let our Ewan know you won't be coming. I can help him with the nets today. You rest up now. Your mam and gran will look after you."

He darted a glance at the two women who smiled faintly, then clattered out of the room, his boots echoing on the stone. There was a bustling at the kitchen door then the sound of it slamming shut.

Cliona stared after him, her mouth agape.

"Who was that and what did he do with my da?"

Helen exchanged another furtive glance with Morag.

"And what's with you two, thick as thieves with all the looks passing between you? What's going on?"

Morag cleared her throat.

Helen spoke.

"Your gran had a word with your da," she said, finally. "She told him…she might have hinted at the reason you fainted was of a womanly nature."

A small smile quirked at the corners of her mouth.

"And your da is a bit queasy on the subject of female matters."

She spread her hands in a gesture of helplessness.

Cliona closed her eyes and groaned aloud.

"I can't believe it," she said, a smile widening on her mouth. "I can't believe you said that. The poor sod will be avoiding me for days."

Her shoulders shook with silent laughter and the two women joined in.

Just then, another stab of pain jabbed behind her eyes. She inhaled sharply and put a hand to her head.

At once, her mam was kneeling beside her.

"Is it happening again?" she asked, her face creased with worry.

She turned to her mother-in-law.

"Surely, she needs a doctor, Morag. We can't let this go on."

Morag shook her head, a sad smile on her lips.

"You know a doctor can't help her, lass. This, as you well know, is something far beyond the world of medicine."

Helen's shoulders sagged, nodding.

"But why is it like this? You said it would just...*happen*, not that it would be so painful for her."

Helen chewed her lip and shot anxious looks at Cliona who was becoming increasingly incredulous.

Morag shook her head.

"It shouldn't be this bad," she acknowledged. "But it could be something to do with the lass herself, she's a scrappy bit, as you know. It could be that she's fighting him."

"Excuse me!" interrupted Cliona, looking between the two women. "I'm *right* here. Would you mind explaining what it is you're on about and why you apparently know the source of my headaches?"

Helen inhaled sharply and pulled back her shoulders. She reached across to tuck the tartan rug more tightly around Cliona but avoided looking her daughter in the eyes.

"Your Gran has something to tell you," she said, without looking up from her ministrations. "But before she does, I want you to know that it's not something we can discuss openly, under any circumstances. Your da....well, your da doesn't hold with the old stories and long ago turned his back on the family heritage."

"Well this sounds ominous," said Cliona, darkly. "Imagine that, more things that da doesn't like or want to talk about. I wouldn't have thought there was anything left."

At that, her mother did look into her eyes.

"Cliona Stewart, you are my only daughter and I thank the Lord every day for giving you to me, after so long wanting you. But," she continued, as Cliona opened her mouth. "But you can be a tiresome harpy with all of your smart mouth and clever quips. You drive your poor da to distraction." She held up a hand, "I know he's a difficult man at the best of times but he loves you just as much as I do and you would do well to remember that and to try and contribute to the peace of this house instead of always riling everyone up."

Cliona bit her lip and looked down at her hands, her face scarlet. It wasn't often her mother had stern words and even more rare that they were directed at Cliona.

"Now," said her mother, giving the rug one last tug, "I'll leave you with your Gran and go and see about getting that bread in the oven. I'm sure it's risen right out of its bowl by now."

As the door to the sitting room gently closed, Cliona let out a shaky breath and sank back against the cushions. She swallowed against the rise of tears in her throat, closing her eyes to stem the ones that had already begun to leak out.

"It's alright, pet," said her gran, coming to perch on the coffee table beside the sofa. She took one of Cliona's hands in her own knobbled fingers, smoothing and patting.

"Your mam worries, that's all. All she wants is a peaceful life and I can't say I blame her. My Donal can be fierce with his temper, he always has been. But as big as his rages are, his heart is bigger still. I know it doesn't excuse the way he treats folk at times, especially the ones that love him best, but that's just the way of it. He's like his own da that way. The streak of temper runs down the male line it seems, just as the wind singing runs down the female one."

Cliona nodded, blinking furiously. It stung more than she

19

wanted to admit knowing that she'd upset her mother. She goaded her da, she knew that, but she couldn't help herself. The words would be out of her mouth before she hardly even knew it herself.

Wait, what?

"What did you just say?" she asked, frowning at her gran who was taking a deep interest in the architecture of the fire in the grate, stabbing at the coals with the poker.

"Hm?"

"Wind singing," repeated Cliona. "What on earth is wind singing?"

"Oh, that," said Morag, waving the poker in the air. Sparks flew off the end of it, momentarily distracting both of them as Morag rushed to stamp out the burners that hit the hearth rug.

"Yes, *that*," said Cliona.

Morag stared into the fire for a few minutes before taking a deep breath, as if preparing for something.

"Are you hearing voices, pet?" asked her gran, changing tack. "Well, not voices in the plural as such, more like just the one. Fellow with a strong, old country sort of accent, like?"

Cliona gaped at her grandmother.

How could she know?

A wave of pain lanced behind her eyes and she closed them, steadying her breath. The now familiar murmuring rumbled inside her mind, like someone speaking from another room.

"I can see by the look on your face that maybe you are," said Morag, her face creasing into a weary smile. The smile was warm and genuine, but it didn't reach her eyes. "Eileen said as much, when I told her you were having the headaches."

"Eileen? Mrs. Glenbogie, you mean? What has she got to do with all of this? Am I the only one who doesn't know anything about my own headaches?"

Cliona felt her colour rising again, only this time because of anger rather than shame.

"Calm yourself, lass. It wasn't anyone's intention to keep anything from you. Only we didn't think…"

"Obviously not," retorted Cliona. "And what about the wind singing, don't try and weasel out of that explanation either."

"Nobody is weaseling, lass," said Morag, her eyes becoming like two pieces of flint. "And I'll remind you of your mam's words. There's no need to go flying off the handle and raging about the place. There's as much of Donal's temper in you as well it seems."

Cliona bit back a sharp response, blowing air out of her nose in frustration.

"I'm sorry, Gran," she said, keeping her tone measured. "I don't want to seem rude or impatient, but you must see it from my point of view. I've spent the last month or so thinking I either had a brain tumour or I was going mad, and sometimes both. And now I hear that not only have my headaches been the topic of great interest but also that it's no surprise to anyone that there's this strange man in my head?"

Morag's eyes widened.

"So you know it's a him, then?" she asked, incredulous.

Cliona frowned and shook her head.

"No. Well, yes. Only not until just now," she said, confused. "I honestly didn't know it was a man until just now. It's been mostly muffled murmurs, like someone far away with cotton wool stuffed in their mouth. I don't know, I just seemed to suddenly realize…"

Her voice tapered off and she sat gazing at the flames, worry flickering across her face. She turned to look at her grandmother, her eyes troubled.

"What is it?" she said, her voice trembling. "What's happening to me?"

"Skelly," said Morag, her voice barely above a whisper. "His name is Skelly."

# Chapter 3

"When had you planned on telling me about all of this? Or maybe you wouldn't have bothered at all. The crippling migraines just interfered with your plans, was that it?"

Cliona poured the boiling water into the teapot, the brown leaves swirling and floating with the current. She set the teapot down on the thistle-shaped trivet in the middle of the scrubbed pine table. Gran and her gran's best friend, Eileen, sat closest to the heat of the ancient Aga, Eileen having not quite embraced the modern convenience of an electric oven.

Morag sighed and glanced sideways at Eileen. The other woman refused to meet her eye, the slice of untouched fruitcake on her plate suddenly requiring intense scrutiny.

"Well?" said Cliona, sitting down in the chair opposite the two elder women. "Are either one of you going to tell me, or do I have figure this all out on my own?" She drummed her fingers on the table and twiddled a butter knife. The Aga hissed and creaked, settling into the task of heating the small kitchen. The pendulum of the wall clock ticked back and forth, its metronome rhythm blending with the soothing silence.

"Mrs. Glenbogie?" said Cliona. The sound of her voice broke the quiet, causing the older woman to flinch. "Gran?"

23

"Och, pet," began Eileen, "It's not that we didn't *want* to tell you, aye? And of course, it all had to come out in the end. It's just a bit…" She splayed her crooked fingers out on the worn surface of the table.

"Complicated," finished her gran.

Cliona nodded thoughtfully. Reaching across the table, she pulled the ladies' teacups toward her and set about filling them from the teapot.

"Right, then," she said, brightly, handing back the cups and pushing the butter dish toward Mrs. Glenbogie. Eileen shifted uncomfortably in her chair like a naughty child about to be dealt her punishment. "If it's that complicated, hadn't we best get on with it?"

\* \* \*

"He's old," began her gran, feebly.

"Oh?" said Cliona, a hint of amusement in her voice. She stirred her spoon around her second cup of tea. The kettle was already on for another pot and she imagined more than a few trips to the privy for all three of them before the telling was finished. The ladies were a tight-lipped pair - the first cup of tea had been dedicated to all of the reasons they *hadn't* forewarned her about Skelly. It had been decided, apparently, between her mam, Gran and Mrs.Glenbogie, that to deny Cliona her chance to go away to university would have been a mistake. So rather than tell her what she needed to know then, as they ought, they waited. Only it seemed they'd waited just a bit too long.

"Well, and harmless enough."

"Relatively speaking, Morag," Mrs. Glenbogie added, giving her friend a remonstrative look.

"Aye, well. It's all relative really, isn't it, Eileen?" she replied, cryptically.

Cliona interrupted their exchange with a sharp, loud rap of the teaspoon on the table.

"Can we just skip ahead to the relevant details, please? Like why I'm hearing this voice in my head and why it's insisting it knows the pair of you?"

The two old ladies paused in stunned silence. They exchanged guilty looks, the unspoken words between them hanging heavily in the air.

Finally, Morag sighed and straightened in her chair. She pulled her shawl tightly around her shoulders and crossed her arms in front of her.

"Fine," she said. "You're right, lass. It's time for the telling."

"Lovely," said Cliona, encouragingly. "Now, he's old. What else? Is he one of the selkies then? The ones we've been collecting the sea glass for all these years. Or was that a load of bollocks too?"

Mrs. Glenbogie's mouth dropped open. She snapped it shut and with a sharp exhale through her nose she turned a fierce and accusing eye toward Morag, who affected a casual air of indifference and flapped her hand in nonchalance.

"What's the matter, Eileen?" she asked, impatiently. "The child needs to know the way of things. I couldn't be sending the wee thing out for the glass without her knowing what she's looking at, now can I? Besides, a bairn needs to be brought up on magic if she's to have any chance in the world."

"But we agreed," replied Eileen through clenched teeth, "that she needed to be older before..."

"Excuse me? Ladies?" interrupted Cliona. "I'm still here, right? And it's a bit late to argue over the When of things, isn't it? What do you think would've happened if Gran hadn't told me about the glass, Mrs. G? Besides, it's not as if anything she told me when I was five at all prepared me for what's happening now. It's not like most people are in the habit of hearing voices, are they? And can you imagine the look on Da's face if I'd told him there was a strange man in my head? Because of Gran's stories and the glass collecting, I've enough sense of the magic in this sodding island to know there's something strange going on. Which, as it happens, is yet another thing about me, apparently, that my father wants nothing to do with.

Eileen Glenbogie snorted in a rather unladylike fashion.

"Your da…"

"Never mind, Eileen," said Morag, quietly but firmly. "There's no need to dredge that up. We've enough troubles without hashing over what we can't change. Donal is a good man. It's not all of us that are meant for this life," She looked pointedly at Eileen who glared back.

"What life?" demanded Cliona, her patience worn thin. "I'm tired of the secrets, Gran. I'm tired of you both treating me like a baby. I'm twenty-four, for god's sake! I've been collecting the glass since I was five! Do you not think it's time you let me into your secret club, or whatever the hell it is the two of you are being so frustratingly cryptic about? And for crying out loud," her voice raised into a shout, "will someone *please* tell me what this wind singing business is all about?"

"Whisht! Cliona," said her gran, reaching across the table to take her granddaughter's hands between her own two. She squeezed them gently and Cliona squeezed back. The two of them sat, holding hands for a moment, eyes locked on one another. Morag squeezed again and let go.

"She's right, Eileen," she said, not taking her eyes from

Cliona's. "It's time we told her what she is."

* * *

"Do you remember, lass, a couple of years ago, there was a bit of storm trouble?" asked her Gran.

Cliona's eyes widened.

"A bit of storm trouble?" she repeated, incredulous. "Is that what you'd call it? I'm assuming you mean the one that killed Joe Ashton, wiped out the electric for a week, wrecked three boats and left Seumas Ferguson's rowboat hanging from the trees? Not to mention the fact that you took ill for a week afterward and Da wouldn't speak to you for a month! Would that be the bit of storm trouble you're referring to?"

Eileen stifled a noise that may have either been laughter or a cough. Morag glared at her with sufficient ferocity to produce her own scowl in return before Eileen addressed Cliona.

"Cliona, pet. The temper doesn't become you. Or at least, it doesn't help, aye?"

"Sorry, Mrs. Glenbogie," said Cliona, her eyes cast down. "It's just that I'm so very frustrated. I feel utterly helpless and it's as if no-one wants to tell me what's going on," She lifted her eyes and looked hard into the elder woman's face. "And then there's the matter of the strange man in my head, you see?"

Morag erupted into an explosion of wheezing laughter.

Grinning, Cliona reached across to hand her a hanky to wipe her eyes.

"Point taken, lass," said Eileen, smiling. "And who knows, mebbe the temper will serve you in the end."

* * *

"I found his particular bit of glass when I was about your age," said Morag, having moved to a worn, wing-backed chair next to the fireplace, her fingers folded lightly around her teacup. "Of course, I hadn't any notion what it was at the time, only that it held a bit more of the feeling, you follow?" She glanced toward Cliona who nodded, shifting slightly in her seat.

Eileen eyed Cliona thoughtfully.

"You *do* know exactly what the glass is, pet?"

Cliona stiffened, blushing.

"Of course I do! I mean, Gran told me when I was little that they were wishes. You know, people made a wish and tossed it into the sea and the selkies would collect them and if the people had been good and kind then they would help the wishes come true. She said we had to collect them to help keep the selkies safe."

She blushed a brighter shade of red. Reciting it back, it sounded juvenile and silly. Five-year-old Cliona, though, had been entranced with the notion that she was helping to keep the selkie magic safe, that she was somehow involved in the mysterious workings of the faery creatures who lived in the sea. As years went by, she'd gone on collecting the glass, never questioning the whys or wherefores of it. It was a habit now, and an excuse to go and walk beside the sea when things at home were difficult. It had been a long time, though, since it felt like something other than yet another chore being demanded of her.

Eileen snorted, turning to Morag who refused to meet her eye.

"Did I not tell you that was a silly idea?"

"Oh?" retorted Morag. "And you think filling a wee bairn's head full of dark magic is a better one, then?"

"Dark magic?" interrupted Cliona, her mouth gone dry.

"Not really dark as in evil, lass," soothed her gran, glaring at Eileen."Although I suppose it is in its way. The Good Folk have their own way of going on and they don't exactly discriminate between 'good' and 'bad' like we do."

"Will you stop talking to the lass as if she's half-witted, Morag?"

Eileen got up from her chair and moved around to where Cliona was sitting. She leaned over her, cupping a knob-jointed hand gently around Cliona's face.

"Cliona, love. You know your Gran means well by you, of course she does. And when you were still a wee thing and we knew you had the gift, we wanted to put it all in a way that made it seem like a game, aye?"

Cliona nodded, dumbly. She had gone from feeling like a foolish child to frightened to confused and then all three jumbled together.

"What your Gran is trying to say, is that we can't put our own values and morals, as it were, onto the Good Folk. They go on by older laws than the ones we made for ourselves. Do you understand that, pet?"

Not waiting for a response, she carried on.

"And so, the ones that live in the sea, well - they're no different. And if we're ever to be dealing with them, we'd do well to remember that."

Morag nodded at Cliona who responded with a small smile.

"Naturally," said Cliona, regaining her composure as she started to put things together. She eyed the two women carefully. "But what occasion we'd need to be having dealings with faery creatures from the sea, I can't quite imagine."

The look that passed over her grandmother's face made her

instantly regret her glib reply. She reached out a hand and put it over Morag's.

"Sorry, Gran. Never mind me, I'm ratty remember? It's just this pounding head and…well, voice," She waved a hand as if to dismiss it all and sighed heavily. "It's all a bit much."

Her gran placed her own hand over Cliona's and gave it a quick squeeze.

"It is that, lassie," she said, glaring over at Mrs.Glenbogie who folded her arms and looked triumphant. "We ought to have told you everything straight from the very start. Nothing good comes from keeping secrets."

"Never mind that, Morag," said Eileen, seizing control of the conversation again, "Don't distract the lass from the point at hand." She nodded at Cliona. "Mistakes were made, pet, that much is true. But it was only for the intention of keeping you safe and letting you live a bit of life. So, let's set that all aside for now, will we?"

Cliona took a deep, steadying breath, forcing down the swelling tide of emotion that was rising in her and nodded, returning the hand-squeeze.

"I understand. I daresay I would have done the same in your position," she said, straightening her shoulders and forcing a bright, brittle smile. "Once again, though, what I don't understand, and would very much like to, is who this Skelly personage is and why he's in my head and does this have anything to do with being a wind singer?"

"Right," said Eileen, narrowing her eyes at her old friend, who barely suppressed a laugh. Cliona may have accepted their excuses, but she wasn't giving up on knowing the details now. "And that's where the glass comes in."

# Chapter 4

"I just feel so *stupid*," said Cliona, hitting out at the long, dune-grass with a stick of driftwood.

"I mean, you just believe people, don't you? Someone you love tells you something when you're little and you just never question it, right? And you just keep *on* believing and never questioning it."

She groaned loudly, thumping the sand with a loud *thwack* .

"Oh, Iain! I am such an enormous *numpty*!"

Iain grinned.

"Ah, that's music to my ears, Cliona Stewart. To think," he flung his arms wide and turned theatrically towards the expanse of sea and sky, "I have borne witness, this very day, to the Great Cliona admitting a state of numptyness!"

He laughed and jumped sideways as Cliona made to thrash him with her driftwood. But she was laughing too and only swung in a half-hearted way. He made a grab for the stick and she let it fall, her shoulders slumping. They shook, gently, with laughter, Iain thought. Soon, though, he realized the laughter had turned to sobs.

"I'm sorry, Clee," he reached out, tentatively, to touch her arm. "I didn't mean…"

She flung his hand away, eyes flashing in her tear-streaked

face.

"Don't you dare!" she cried.

Iain stepped back, hurt and confused.

"What? I just…"

"No! Don't you ever be anything but what you are, do you hear me? Don't you ever, *ever* tell me lies!"

With that, she spun around and started running.

She ran until her chest ached and a sharp stitch pierced her left side. She stumbled to a halt and sank down to her knees in the sand. The tears had long dried, leaving stiff, salty streaks down her cheeks. Her throat was raw as she gasped for air and her skin felt tight and ragged

She felt him arrive, rather than heard him. The sand muffled his footsteps to nothing more than a shifting of grains underneath his boots. But they'd been friends since they were four and her gran had always told her that the two of them were old souls, companions from another life, even.

He stood quietly behind her for a while before clearing his throat.

"Cliona?"

She didn't speak, but turned her head slightly, in acknowledgment of his words, giving him permission to go on.

"I know it's me who's the chronic numpty, I can't help it. But I've never told you lies, and I never will, right? We promised that when we were just bairns and I wouldn't ever go back on my word. I'm a lot of things, Clee, but I'm not a liar. And I especially wouldn't go lightly with what you are and what…"

"I know," said Cliona, quietly. "I'm sorry, Iain. I shouldn't've taken it out on you. I'm being embarrassingly theatrical. It's just, this is all *wrong*! I don't *want* this, Iain. I don't. Don't you see? Knowing this changes everything. What about my life?

What about the things I was meant to be doing?"

Her shoulders slumped and she began weeping again, tears of anger and frustration. She grabbed handfuls of sand and threw them. The grains caught the strengthening breeze and fanned out into a great arc before settling back to join the trillions of other grains on the beach.

Tentatively, Iain reached out again to touch her shoulder. When she leaned slightly towards his touch, he knelt down behind her. He wrapped his arms around her shuddering form while the gulls keened in the rising wind.

They sat, huddled together, for what seemed like ages. Iain's right arm had gone to sleep but he dared not move lest he break the silence into which Cliona had eventually fallen. The wind had turned to sharp gusts, whipping up dervishes of sand and carrying the scent of fish and salt and seaweed into their faces.

Eventually, Cliona spoke.

"I don't want this, Iain," she repeated, quietly but matter-of-factly. "I didn't ask to be part of this, and feeling like I've been played a fool all these years? Well, that just tops it all off, you know? And now this…this…. *person*, if you could really call him that? This person is just suddenly there, in my head, and I've no choice in the matter? I had plans, Iain. I was going to get that internship in Paris. I was going to travel the world. So many things…and now this."

Iain sighed.

"Did they tell you why he just waltzed into your head? I mean, is there a reason why he arrived just now, of all times. Is there another storm coming?"

His voice faltered a little at the last question. They'd only witnessed one of the faery storms in their life so far, but it was enough to know they were something to dread.

33

"I don't know about a storm, exactly, but Gran said he came to me for the sole reason that I'm next in line for the honour of his assistance."

Iain chuckled. "Did your gran actually say that?"

"No, silly. That's just me, adding my own ratty twist," replied Cliona, easing herself out of Iain's arms and turning to face him. "The pair of them were just so bloody casual about the whole thing. They just assumed I'd be quite alright with having been told childish stories all these years and that I'd happily carry on like I was desperately glad for the experience. They thought that since I'd gone away to school and done my degree that I'd be quite delighted to settle back here in Glencarragh to knit jumpers and mend fishing nets the rest of my life. A gift, they call it. I don't know about your definition of a gift, but this certainly falls short of my expectations."

Iain rubbed feeling back into his arm and smiled.

"Well, I can't say it tops my list, either. But it's good to see you're getting your piss and vinegar back. I don't think I can manage Sobby Cliona very often. She's very hard on my arms."

He stood up, shaking the sand from his jeans and reached out his hands, pulling Cliona to her feet. She laughed and punched him gently in the arm.

"There, that's better," he said, reaching out to pull a piece of seaweed out of her hair. He waved it at her, grinning. "You're starting to look like one of them, already, yeah?"

Cliona frowned.

"Please don't joke about it, Iain," she begged. "I need you to be serious for just a bit, right?"

"Right. Sorry, I'll promise to keep a grip on my inner numpty for as long as you need me to," he said, schooling his face into seriousness.

Smiling, Cliona sighed. "Thank you, Iain. I don't know that I'll manage this without you, I really don't."

"What've you got to manage then? Did they tell you what your new friend wants?"

He laughed at the look of surprise on her face.

"Well, of course the conniving sod must want something," he said, shrugging with the casual acceptance of someone having grown up with the magical realities of the island. "Don't they always? There's not a faery in the world that ever does a thing out of the goodness of their heart."

\* \* \*

"Do you ever wonder what it'd be like if we'd grown up somewhere else?" asked Cliona.

The two of them had started walking, an unspoken need to move, to talk but to not have to look one another in the eye as they did so.

"I suppose," said Iain, shrugging. "I imagine everyone here does that sometimes - you know, imagine how it'd be to live in a normal place, somewhere not over-run with lunatic sea creatures and wild women married to the north wind."

He elbowed Cliona softly at her swift intake of breath beside him.

"You said yourself that you didn't want me to be anything other than what I am, right? And what I am is a cheeky-mouthed pain in your arse, yeah?"

She smiled.

"Aye, that you are, Iain. That you are."

The sky was a leaden grey. Dark clouds skittered across

the horizon, forming and dissipating, looming black and then retreating in the same rhythm of the water creeping back and forth across the sand.

"But what I mean is, do you ever wish you didn't *know* about any of this?" she swung an arm in gesture toward the moody sea and the menacing sky. "Do you ever wonder what it would be like to just get up in the morning and make a cup of tea and head out to a job? Can you imagine not having the weight of it all…"

Shaking her head, she left the thought unfinished.

Iain sighed, pushing his hands deeper into the pockets of his pea coat, hunching his shoulders against the gusting wind.

"Aye, I do," he said. "But wondering about it isn't going to change much, is it? This is what we've got, so we've no choice but to manage, haven't we?"

"Haven't we, though?" she asked, stopping to stare out across the stretch of wet sand.

The tide was going out, leaving clumps of seaweed and bits of wood and litter - things cast off and purged, things which didn't belong. The sea had a way of ridding itself of the alien, of unwanted things. She briefly thought of Skelly and his people, no longer welcome in the place that had been their home for an eternity. How must it feel, she wondered, to be so adrift? So without?

"I suppose you can't really blame your one, Skelly, though, can you?" said Iain, as if reading her thoughts. "I think I'd do anything to protect the people I care about. Most people would."

"Even when it means the loss of one soul to save another?"

She brought her gaze from the horizon toward the face of her oldest friend.

"Aye," whispered Iain, his black eyes looking into her green ones. "If that's what it came to."

# Chapter 5

"The selkies weren't always as we know them, right?"

The three women had been well into the second pot of tea before the information finally started flowing. "They didn't always have the ability to walk the land, to shed their skin and be like humans, you see."

Cliona nodded. She stood with her back to the two women, having been pressed into frying some bacon for tea. It made it easier, anyway. She felt an utter fool. She was also starting to get just a tiny bit angry again and she didn't want them to see it showing on her face.

"I know. You told me that one when I was little, Gran. The story about the forest-god and his bride."

Morag beamed at Eileen.

"See, you silly old hen. I told you I'd manage it in my own way."

Mrs. Glenbogie scowled and made a tutting sound in the back of her throat.

"Anyway, lass. To cut a long story short, because of what went on between those two, there were others of the sea who thought they, too, would like the gift of land-walking. But, as it goes, in order for them to have that, they had to give something up in return."

"The balance, yes," said Cliona, transferring some of the rashers to a plate and dabbing at them with a bit of paper towel. "One of the few laws of Faery, I remember."

"Oh! Would you mind heating up a tin of tomatoes to go with that, love?" asked Eileen. "I just fancy a bit of tomato with the bacon, I think. And maybe a bit of mushroom fried, eh, Morag?"

"Oh, aye. That'd be grand. I've had nothing since breakfast."

Cliona gritted her teeth.

"Yes, of course," she muttered. "Nothing would make me happier."

"What's that pet?"

"Nothing, Gran. Carry on, will you? You said the selkies had to give something up?"

"Right. Yes. Well, they started off as the elementals, of course, or merrin as we know them now. They were part of the sea in such a way that they ought not to have been able to manage to survive on the land. Your Skelly, though, being a ruler of his folk, had the power to allow them to go land-walking for bits at a time if that's what they wanted. But, and this is where it gets complicated, not all of the merrin thought that was a good idea. There was a particular faction that felt the sea-folk ought never to mingle with land-walkers, mortals you see. They believed it was a taint on the rest of them."

"Charming," murmured Cliona. "Sea supremacists."

"What's that, love?"

Cliona shook her head.

"Nothing, carry on."

"So, the leader of that lot, to whom your Skelly just so happened to be consort, a right horrible piece calling herself Lira, took against him for what he'd allowed and had him and his folk flung out of the sea. Only she didn't do it completely, for some reason. Who knows, I suppose maybe even she had some scruples. Anyroad, Skelly was fully exiled, but the punishment of his folk was to be trapped between the land and sea for eternity."

"And that's how selkies were born?"

Eileen stifled a giggle.

"There's no need for your sarcasm, madam," said Morag, her eyes flashing.

Cliona ignored the comment and carried on.

"Let me see if I've got the gist this. For Skelly's people - and I'll thank you to stop referring to him as mine, by the way - to be able to walk on land and mingle with the humans, for them to have that ability, they had to lose part of what made them as they were, as elementals?"

"That's it, lass. It's why they have to leave their skin behind when they're ashore. Because they need to be vulnerable on land," put in Morag, smiling benignly at Eileen. "And when they're in the sea, they're bound into a seal form, unable to fully *be* in their world, as they once were. Essentially, Lira trapped them in a state that was only meant for a temporary diversion.

"The merrin are near invincible," said Eileen, scowling at Morag, "just as long as they're in their natural element. It only followed that they couldn't be that way on land. It's all part of the balancing of things - you can't have one thing without leaving go of another."

"But what's that to do with the sea glass?" asked Cliona, wearily, scraping sliced mushroom (and a bit of onion, because she knew from experience that'd be the next request) into the cast iron pan. "The skin thing makes sense, but I don't see how…"

Eileen held up a hand.

"Patience, child! You've always got to be rushing things along. 'Tis a treacherous flaw in young people these days, Morag," she said, turning to her friend who just shrugged and grinned at the sight of Cliona's shoulders stiffening. "They just can't wait to be galloping off to the next thing before the first thing is barely started."

"Aye well, Eileen. I seem to recall a certain young lass who ended up on her arse in the tide-pools thinking she could sing a merrin to her own vain self before she even knew what it would've meant if she'd managed it."

Cliona stifled a giggle, covering up the sound by stirring the tomatoes around the saucepan with a metal spoon.

"Hmph!" came the response. "Anyway, as I was about to say before I was interrupted…"

"Right you are, carry on," said Morag, smiling encouragingly, ignoring the glare from Eileen.

"…the glass is what was left behind when they were changed. Sort of a magical leftover, if you like, from the transformation. 'Tisn't really glass, as such, after all. Each piece holds a wee fragment of what each creature used to be."

"Which is why it has a different feel to it?" asked Cliona, her back still turned to the two women.

"Exactly! Just as there are seals and there are selkies, there's actual sea glass, and there's the selkie's glass!" finished Eileen, turning triumphantly to Cliona's gran. "You see, Morag? The child's no half-wit. You should've told her all this ages ago; we'd've saved a lot of bother when Himself turned up."

"And where exactly does 'Himself' come into all of this?" said Cliona, a hint of something like fury in her voice. "Which is to say, why is he not just off somewhere living out his punishment

41

instead of disrupting my life?" She had turned to face them and stood with a hand on her hip, the spatula raised and dripping bacon grease.

Eileen flapped a hand dismissively, avoiding Cliona's fierce green eyes.

"Och, lass. Don't agitate yourself, I was getting to him," she shifted uncomfortably in her chair, glancing briefly at Morag who was busying herself smoothing down the curling edge of a crocheted placemat.

Clearing her throat, she said quietly. "Apart from being who he is in himself, he's what you might call a benefactor, aye? Sort of a helping hand, as it were. We like to think of him as providing a bit of assistance in the matter of a mutual interest…"

The spatula landed on the Aga with a clatter. Cliona stood with folded arms and a fierce scowl. The two women sat, quietly avoiding her accusing glare, like two recalcitrant children. The bacon fizzled and popped in the frying pan and the tomatoes glubbed and bubbled.

"Are you telling me you're in cahoots with this…this…creature?" She looked from one to the other, settling her eyes on her gran. "After everything you told me about them? All of your stories, all of your instructions. After every promise you made me promise? That you don't ever, under any circumstance…"

"…ever strike a bargain with a faery," finished Morag with a heavy sigh. "Aye, well. Sometimes you just can't predict the pressing nature of certain circumstances."

Eileen nodded sagely. She got up from her chair and went to stand beside her old friend. Placing her hands on the other woman's shawl-clad shoulders, she gave them a small squeeze. Morag reached up and placed her hand on top of Eileen's.

"Especially when it comes to a choice between life and death."

\* \* \*

"I knew straight away that it wasn't just an ordinary bit of the selkie glass," Morag explained. "Here, lass, have a bit of toast, aye? You've barely touched your food. You need your strength, now tuck in."

The three of them sat around the kitchen table. The clink and clatter of forks on plates settled the mood into companionable silence as Cliona had dished up the meal. Setting out the plates and filling the teapot (how much tea had they drunk?) helped to return the atmosphere to one of blissful normalcy. One could almost imagine it was three ordinary people in an ordinary kitchen having an ordinary conversation over bacon sandwiches and fried mushrooms.

Eileen had lit the oil lamps to chase away the rising dark. The glow of them softened the sharp edges of the room and harried the shadows gathering at the edges.

"It had a stronger feel to it, that particular bit of glass. You know how some of them are more full of the feeling than others?"

Cliona nodded, her eyes down. Her stomach in knots, she just pushed the food around her plate.

"Well, to cut a long story, it was Himself as was the beginning of it all."

Cliona looked up.

"Beginning of what?"

"The selkies, like. It was him as made it so they changed from themselves - as the sea-elementals, the merrin - into the selkies."

43

Cliona waved her knife, impatient.

"Yes, I know, I know. We've been over that."

"Keep your hair on, lass, and let me finish. So, you remember the story I told you as a wee bairn? The one about the lord of the sea and his daughter?"

"Yes, of course."

"Well, our one - Skelly, is the name he uses now - is that one very same lord of the sea in the story."

Cliona's eyes widened.

Her gran nodded. She reached for another slice of bread which she slowly buttered. Cliona's fingers clenched her skirt into bunches, willing herself not to scream at the impatience that was bubbling like fury in her chest.

"Well, that whole lark about the battle between him and the forest-god? 'Tis more or less true. Such as he told me and such as you can ever believe a word the feckless shite..."

"Morag!" exclaimed Eileen. "Really! 'Tis no way..."

"Och, never mind, Eileen. It's not as if she hasn't lived around fishermen all her life."

Cliona suppressed a smile.

"Anyway, the gist of the story is that what he did — letting his daughter go land-side and taking the north wind from the forest-god in return — well, 'twas a terrible liberty. And that's what gave his folk the want of the land, you see? Like a temptation that they hadn't had before. And like I said, when the wee bastards..."

Eileen cleared her throat loudly and clattered the butter dish.

Cliona grinned.

"...when the wee bastards," repeated Morag, "took it into themselves that they fancied trying out the land for themselves, it was an awful trial to try and turn them from it. They wanted it and that was that. And so it was Himself that was punished for it. The elementals are the most ancient of them all. They've no notion at all of what it's like beyond their own world and they couldn't care less for any of it. Not like your brownies and piskies and such, the ones that live among us and need us to believe in them. The elementals will carry on regardless."

"And so, when Skelly, by letting his daughter go land-side, showed his folk the other side of things," explained Eileen, filling Morag's teacup, "Have a drop, pet. You'll be parched with all the talking. Let me take over for a bit, aye?"

Eileen settled herself back in her chair, stifling a belch. "Anyway, once they saw it, they wanted it and even though he tried to turn them from the idea, they wouldn't have it. It was fairly much their ending. At least, as far as the merrin were concerned, because, as I said before, some of them - Lira's lot - they'd not tolerate any creature with the taint of the land on them. So they were all cast out."

"But so what? They can still live in the sea, can't they? As selkies. And what about Skelly? asked Cliona.

"Aye well, there's the thing," said Eileen. "Sure, the selkies can *live* in the sea, but they're not truly *of* the sea anymore. Not like they were, anyway. Does that make sense, lass? And they don't belong on the land, either. It's like they're..."

"Torn between the two worlds," whispered Cliona. "I see."

Morag frowned at her granddaughter.

"And Skelly?" continued Eileen. "That's the rub of it. He was banished altogether. He can't come anywhere near the sea; it's desperate agony for him if he does and not only that, it runs the risk of bringing Lira out after him. She's sworn to finish him off if she catches him."

"Aye," added Morag, "and to make it even worse, it's sure

death for his selkie-folk."

"Why?"

"They're drawn to him, aye? He's their lord, after all."

"Was," corrected Morag.

"Right. *Was* their lord," said Eileen. "And if he draws them out, they'll no' go back without him. And for them to stay on the land for too long, well, it drains their magic; their life force, I suppose it is. That's why he stays away."

"And the glass? What about Skelly's glass?"

"Aye, well," sighed Morag. "That was the saving of us, that was."

# Chapter 6

"You're back again? That's two days in a row now. People will start to talk. They'll think you're actually one for the island life."

Ewan's mouth quirked into an amused smile. His hands were buried in the mechanism of a net winch and he was covered in grease up to his elbows.

"You forgot your dinner," said Cliona, waving a paper bag. "Like the half-wit you are."

Ewan grinned, teeth white against the dark smudges of dirt and oil on his face.

"Och, but aren't I just fortunate to have a guardian angel to look after me, then? Isn't that what they say? The good Lord looks after fools and children? Or is it drunks? I can never remember."

"Heathen," scolded Cliona, mockingly. She started to walk around the boat shed, fingers trailing on the neatly stacked piles of nets. "Anyway, don't get excited. I only wanted to get out of the house. Da and Gran were winding up into one of their barneys and Iain is off at some meeting about the boat tours."

She shot a glance at Ewan at the mention of the boat tours, but he was in deep concentration and there was no evidence on his face that he'd heard her.

She let him work in silence for a moment.

"Is it working yet?" she asked, coming to stand beside him. She peered into the tangle of gears and cable. It never failed to amaze her that her brother knew his way around such things, having never been formally taught.

Ewan shook his head.

"No, well, at least not in the way I want it to. I want to be able to adjust the tension more easily, aye? Make it more like a fishing rod, where you can ease up then let it go. I feel like it'll be bit kinder that way. It'll make it easier to sort through the catch. No sense disturbing things that don't need disturbing."

He looked up from his work, his eyes sparkling with enthusiasm. Fishing didn't light him up the way tinkering with mechanical things did, thought Cliona. That's what he ought to be doing with himself.

She nodded, biting her lip.

Another of the many arguments that went around the kitchen table was that of fishing ethics. Ewan was convinced that kinder fishing practices would be the solution to the shrinking populations and was trying to modify the spare winch to support his theory. Donal Stewart thought it was a load of bollocks and hadn't Glencarragh fishermen been doing it the same way for centuries and the lower fish populations were down to a government conspiracy which allowed foreign boats too close to the traditional island waters. Morag asserted that it was faery meddling and both Helen and Cliona barely gave it much thought at all.

"You'll sort it," she said, fully convinced of it. "The winter is long," she intoned, mimicking the oft-repeated phrase of the older fishermen, "and the nets always need mending."

Ewan chuckled.

"And since I've got you to mend the nets, I can spend my time tinkering with my inventions."

"So you think," said Cliona, aiming a mock slap at his arm. "Who knows, maybe I have greater destinies than mending fishing nets?"

Ewan's face clouded over.

"You don't really believe all that stuff Gran and Mrs. Glenbogie have told you? All that wind singing nonsense?"

Cliona blushed.

"You're starting to sound like Da," she said, fighting with an unexpected surge of disappointment. She may not have liked how Morag and Eileen had handled the situation, but a small part of her was beginning to recognize a strange sense of pride in feeling she was apparently part of something bigger and more exciting than the mundane days currently offered by Glencarragh life. Besides, she hadn't been referring to that at all. Her destiny, she had thought, lay elsewhere.

Ewan shrugged, returning to his tinkering.

"I suppose," he said. "But you'd be far better off seeing a doctor for those headaches."

Cliona swallowed a sharp retort. She had told her brother about everything but Skelly. Her instinct had warned her that would have been a step too far. That, in itself, had wounded her slightly. She didn't like to think there was a part of herself of which Ewan would disapprove.

"I will," she said, keeping her tone light. "Besides, I was referring to my future life as world traveler and woman of adventure."

Ewan snorted.

"Never you mind," she said, still speaking jokingly but

genuinely stung. "Don't you know you're supposed to tread softly?"

"What?"

Ewan's voice was muffled, his head deep inside the inner workings of the engine.

*"But I, being poor, have only my dreams; I have spread my dreams under your feet; Tread softly because you tread on my dreams,"* she whispered.

"Nothing," she said, raising her voice. "Don't forget to eat. I made rock buns this morning and saved you the best ones."

"Ta, pet," came the reply.

Cliona paused, looking at the figure of her brother bent over the workings of his latest project, seeing him sink into the sort of oblivion that comes with being fully immersed in something beloved. It was the kind of feeling she got when she was taking apart a discarded piece of clothing or fabric and re-imagining it into something beautiful. Some days, there was nothing she wanted more than to be able to fit in; to be the sort of person who could love island life as much as her brother did. After all, he didn't always follow the status quo; even amid the restrictions of duty and family he'd found his own way and why couldn't she?

A gust of wind whistled through the window frame and a sudden blast of rain clattered on the metal roof like a handful of thrown pebbles.

Ewan raised his head, frowning.

"Sounds like the weather's winding up again," he said, glancing over at the window. "Strange, the forecast called for it clearing."

Cliona grunted.

"You should know by now that the weather on Glencarragh

doesn't follow any forecast."

She immediately regretted the bitterness in her tone.

Ewan looked at her, his gaze steady. She met his eyes, challenging. He looked away first and she felt her heart sink.

"Thanks again for dropping my dinner by. I'll be ready for it when I'm finished with this lot."

"Right," she said, understanding that she was being dismissed. "I'll be off, then."

She tried to close the door quietly, but a gust of wind grabbed it from her hands and it crashed shut.

"Great," she muttered. "That'll do nothing to dissuade him that I'm a bad-tempered beast."

*Aren't you, then?*

Cliona staggered in the force of the wind, clutching her mackintosh around her as it tried to flap its way to freedom.

*I'm not listening to you,* she replied. *And I would appreciate you sodding right off.*

She'd been hearing Skelly's voice clearly for a few days. He popped in, she'd explained to Iain, usually at the most inconvenient moments and usually with a commentary on her bad manners or poor behaviour.

*Aye, well. I think we both know I can't do that.*

*Do we know that, though?* she replied, almost forgetting not to speak aloud. She'd done that a few times, garnering strange looks and no doubt feeding the Glencarragh gossip machine for days. *Do we really? Because I'm more than happy to end this right now so don't hang about on my account. Whatever business you have with Mrs. Glenbogie and my gran is nothing to do with me. As far as I'm concerned, we have nothing further to discuss.*

Blessed silence.

There, she thought. That shut him up. Odious creature.

She concentrated on making her way to the bookshop. If Iain wasn't around, perhaps Feargus would stand her a cup of tea and a commiserating ear.

The wind tore through the narrow streets, sending shop awnings billowing; the few other folk who were brave enough to be out had their heads down, shopping bags clutched to them. Despite the rain, there was no point in umbrellas as they were a favourite of the wind. You could always spot the tourists on the first day of their visit; they were the ones carrying umbrellas. On the second day, they simply huddled into their hoods like everyone else. When they were younger, Cliona and Iain made up elaborate tales of another island, just downwind of Glencarragh, where all of the umbrellas ended up. Predictably enough, it was called The Island of Lost Umbrellas. It had entertained them for weeks.

She was thinking of the umbrella island when Skelly's voice returned to her consciousness.

*It may be that you want none of this,* he said. *And I can understand why. But the truth of it is, neither of us have a choice in the matter. We're bound together by old stories and older promises. The sooner you accept that, the better off we'll all be. There's a storm rising, lass. You'll be wanted.*

Cliona gritted her teeth, against the cold wind and the voice in her head.

*I accept nothing,* she said. *And you don't need me. You've got my gran and Mrs. Glenbogie. They know what they're doing and more importantly, they've bought into this whole ridiculous tale. I, however, have other things to do. Now kindly bugger off. I want to visit my friend and I've no desire to come off like a raving lunatic.*

Leaning into the wind, she arrived at the blue-painted door of The Oracle, the odd little bookshop belonging to one of

52

Glencarragh's most beloved off-islanders.

Feargus MacLeary had been a bastion of the repertory theatre scene for several highly acclaimed decades before, somewhat inexplicably at first, retiring to Glencarragh. He'd opened up his crooked little shop that dealt in used and rare books, along with other oddments, and it had fast become a favourite of tourists and natives alike. He'd raised more than a few eyebrows when he'd first arrived, his penchant for waistcoats and tweed plus-fours startled the more conventional inhabitants of the island. But his good nature and generosity soon won them over and he'd been welcomed into the community in a way that off-islanders rarely were. This innate reserve had less to do with any unfriendliness of Glencarragh folk and more to do with the fact it was very rare for people to come and live on the island voluntarily and so were viewed with careful suspicion at first. There was no point, so the local wisdom stated, in getting attached to folk that might just up and go again once the place got at them.

The sign was still turned to the 'closed' side, but Cliona knew that was mostly a formality. She checked her watch. It was just after eleven. Perfect timing.

She reached up and turned the old-fashioned bell. It jangled somewhere deep in the catacombs that made up the bookshop.

Feargus also had a fondness for collecting "bits of things", like old biscuit tins and aged garden implements; these collections tended to line the passageways before mysteriously disappearing in a steady stream of acquisition and dispersement. Iain's theory was that the cultured, slightly snobbish shopkeeper frequented car boot sales on the mainland, a pastime that seemed far less likely than Cliona's suggestion that he was selling worthless, battered biscuit tins found in people's sheds and attics to the tourists for exorbitant prices.

"Coming!" came a voice from inside the shop. A torrent of profanity followed a loud crash and the offended yowl of a cat. Malcolm was another oddity of Feargus'. He'd been a moth-eaten looking stray that had appeared in the vicinity of the dustbins shortly after the shop opened. Clumps of long, yellowy-beige fur wadded into giant mats and a perpetually runny nose had made him an unattractive option for the fastidious Feargus. Somehow, though, the two had become fast friends and it wasn't long before Malcolm had free run of the shop and the little flat above it. His fur was now clean and despite allowing himself to be combed regularly, years of matted fur had left him with bald and thinning patches on his coat, creating a look of permanent dishevelment; several courses of antibiotics hadn't been able to completely sort out his runny nose and so it was simply accepted as part of his charm.

The door yanked open and a slightly rumpled Feargus stood in the doorway. His great mass of wav, white hair had escaped its usual meticulous coiffure and his spotted bow tie hung askew.

"Cliona!" he said, beaming. He promptly turned on his heel and started back down the passageway, talking to her over his shoulder. It was just assumed she'd follow. "How are you this fine morning? Pardon my state, I've been crawling about in the attic looking for a book someone off the mainland wants and the place is a veritable maze of chaos. I'll just put the kettle on. Come on in and tell me everything."

Cliona smiled to herself. That was Feargus all over and one of the reasons he was so popular. He would happily drop everything for a mug of tea and a chat. She had a strong suspicion that the shop was simply something he kept up to pass the time, rather than a necessity to support himself. Which was fortunate, as the market for dented cake tins and rare books on Glencarragh wasn't all that large.

She made her way down the passage, wending through the stacks of biscuit tins and galvanized pails. A set of wooden handled garden shears leaned precariously against a tower of coal scuttles. That must be what just fell, she mused, settling the shears into a sturdier arrangement. Malcolm perched on top of a stack of ancient Country Living magazines, regarding her blearily. He sneezed, sending a spray across the magazines. Cliona winced.

"Hello, Malcolm. Lovely to see you, as always,"

She reached up to gingerly stroke the bedraggled cat, who received her attentions with mild disdain. He blinked slowly, acknowledging her worthiness. Having satisfied the gate-keeper, Cliona by-passed the door leading to Feargus' flat and went into the little shop.

A smell of beeswax and lemon mingled with the musty scent of old paper and Cliona took a deep, fortifying breath, feeling the tension of the past few weeks melting away.

She followed the whistle of the kettle, walking behind the massive, carved oak table that served as the checkout area, complete with old-fashioned cash register, to part a, slightly balding, green velvet curtain that hid a small anteroom. Feargus had kitted this little cubbyhole out with a gas-bottled hob and all the necessary tea-making accoutrements. To the eye, it seemed a small, cramped space, but somehow, no matter how many people were in there, it never felt crowded.

Feargus bustled about, spooning tea into a large, Victorian china teapot, patterned with cabbage roses. He wouldn't entertain the convenience of bags and always served the brew in china teacups, the idea of tea in a mug offending his cultured sensibilities. Cliona found teacups to be fiddly and unsatisfyingly small, but the former thespian was not to be convinced.

"Standards!" he'd lectured herself and Iain once, when they'd argued the case for a grand big mug of tea. "It's what you young people are sorely lacking these days. Standards and decorum. The preservation of manners and polite society, that's what this is really about...."

He'd gone on at great length and the two young people had learned their lesson. Tea in china cups was the price to pay for Feargus' hospitality. But it was worth it.

"Ta, Feargus," said Cliona, accepting the offered cup. She attempted to warm her hands around the delicate china, to little success.

"Perishing out there, isn't it my girl?" said Feargus, viewing her red cheeks and damp hair. "I'm afraid we're in for another one."

Cliona kept her eyes down and gave a noncommittal grunt. The last thing she wanted to do was discuss the weather.

Feargus regarded her thoughtfully. His smooth, unlined face was in sharp contrast to his mop of white hair and his bright blue eyes missed nothing.

"Are you able for it, then?" he asked, finally deciding he might as well get it over with. "Will you sing the wind?"

# Chapter 7

"How do you know about all this?" Cliona asked, wiping the tea from her chin where she'd almost spat her mouthful across the little room. They were each perched on the high wooden stools that Feargus kept in the little anteroom for visitors. Malcolm had wandered in, stertorous breathing filling the awkward silence as Cliona cleaned herself up. Feargus looked helpfully away as she did so.

"Well?" she repeated, once decorum had been regained.

Feargus shrugged, waving a dismissive hand.

"I've lived a lot of places, my girl. I've seen a lot of things, much of which most folk wouldn't believe. It's why I came to your blessed isle, I wanted to live in a place where the folk *do* believe in improbable things."

Cliona stared at him. He smoothed a hand over his yellow and brown tartan waistcoat. He looks like Rupert the bear, she thought absently. Pulling herself back to the subject at hand, she said,

"And that answers my question, how?"

Feargus grinned, showing a row of even, white teeth. His blue eyes twinkled merrily.

"I believe it answers it quite satisfactorily," he said. "Biscuit?"

He offered a plate, piled high with Garibaldi biscuits. Scowling, Cliona helped herself to a couple. He knew they were her favourite.

"You've been talking to Gran and Mrs. Glenbogie, then?" she said, munching.

Feargus simply smiled.

"Those dear ladies and I are frequently together for tea and conversation, yes."

Cliona sighed; she wasn't going to get a straight answer.

"It doesn't matter, anyway," she said, starting on her second biscuit.

"Oh?"

"Because I'm having none of it. They don't need me and I've no interest at all in embroiling myself in any further lunacy associated with this bloody island. The wind can blow it off the map for all I care."

Feargus nodded, sipping his tea.

"You're still planning on doing a bunk, then?"

"I'm not 'doing a bunk', Feargus. You make it sound so…so underhanded. It's not like I'm going to run off and not tell anyone."

"And that makes it different?"

"Of course it does! Don't be so pedantic. Everyone knows that I have plans."

"And they don't include helping two old women battle a deadly faery storm?"

"Feargus!"

Cliona flushed scarlet and was furious to realize there were tears welling in her eyes.

"Don't say it like that," she said, her voice cracking.

The weight of expectation and obligation was bearing down

on her. She'd tried repeatedly, since learning of her alleged heritage, to justify her refusal to accept the immense responsibility which had suddenly been thrust upon her. She'd managed quite well to set it all aside, but something about the way Feargus had simplified it brought the whole unimaginable thing rushing back.

"But that's what it is, isn't it, lass?" said Feargus, his voice soft and his eyes filled with compassion.

"They need your help, my darling girl."

Cliona shook her head, not wanting it to be true but knowing, deep down that it was.

"They can't do it alone. Not anymore."

* * *

"So you've found it, then. What's left of me."

His voice had been bitter. And sad.

"Aye, I have. And so, what does that mean?"

Morag sounded braver than she felt. She clutched the worn stone in her hand, inside the pocket of the flowered pinny that her mam had helped her to sew when she was only twelve. She'd worn it, even though it was starting to be too small, hoping that the spirit of her mam, sewn into the very fabric, would give her the strength to do what needed doing.

The rain had started, stuttering in fat droplets on the sharp-edged rocks as the sea roiled across the sand, building in ferocity, a steady punishing of the land for its existence.

"That depends," he'd answered, wincing with the effort of standing so close to the sea. "You've called me with it. I suppose that means you mean to do something with me."

Morag regarded the creature standing before her. Tall, strangely beautiful, but with a harsh edge to his sharp-featured face.

Sorrow, she thought, it was sorrow that etched the lines around his slanted green-gold eyes.

"The storms are starting again," she said, "and I don't think I can manage…"

Her voice broke then, fear and fatigue breaking through the brave façade she'd tried to cultivate when she'd decided to summon whomever the glass belonged to. Eileen had begged her not to, tried to convince her that they'd be able to sing the wind, just the two of them; Morag for the song and Eileen as her anchor. But this would be the first storm without her mother. The grief of that was twofold; the loss of her mother, and the inevitable losses that the storms would bring if she couldn't sing the wind.

"My mother," she began, still faltering.

"Aye, I know," he answered. "I know who you are. You and yon black-haired lassie."

"What?" Morag spun around to see Eileen crawling out from behind the cluster of rocks that lay scattered behind them on the beach. She was pulling strands of seaweed from her hair and brushing the sand from the creases of her dress.

"Well!" she snorted, in response to Morag's questioning look. "I couldn't very well let you get on by your own foolish self, could I?" Her black eyes flashed but she gripped her friends elbow in a quick squeeze of affection. Her fingers were wet and ice cold. "You're the one then, aye?" she said to the tall faery who stood, streaming rain and agony and loss in front of them.

"I am," he replied stiffly. "What will you have of me, then?

60

Quick as you can, before they come."

Morag and Eileen stood side by side, hands clasped together, young faces contorted with an agony of their own. Unspoken between them, the promises and warnings of the generations of women that had come before.

*The wind singers work alone; they may use only the magic they harvest themselves. As well, they may choose an anchor - a companion of the soul to hold and shelter them.*

*Take what the sea offers freely, nothing more. It is enough.*

"But it won't be enough," Morag had argued to Eileen. "We're not strong enough. And this storm? This storm is bigger. It's like it knows...it knows me mam isn't here."

"Hush, pet," Eileen had soothed, as her friend broke into desperate sobs.

Morag glanced at Eileen, who nodded, imperceptibly.

Pulling the glass out of her pinny pocket, she held it out to the once-lord of the sea.

"Take it," she said, her voice whipped away by the rising keen of the wind. Not that it mattered, she could already hear him in her mind. It had worked.

"At what price?" he asked.

"Your promise for ours," she replied, praying silently to the ghost of her mother for forgiveness. "Our protection for yours."

He stared at them for a moment.

Calculating, she thought.

The lines of strain were deepening along his beautiful face. The rain streaked through the ropes of his green-blue hair and his long fingers clenched and unclenched. The sea roared more loudly behind them, joining the wind in its assault upon the shore.

"Agreed," he said. "We have a bargain."

His hand closed over the polished stone in hers. A shudder-ing warmth shot up her arm like a jolt of electricity.

Eileen held her up as her knees gave way.

"Get away wi' ye!" she shouted above the howling wind as Morag collapsed in a heap on the sand.

\* \* \*

Cliona battled the gusting wind as she made her way slowly home. Her visit to Feargus hadn't been the refuge she'd thought it would be. In the end, they'd chatted of inconsequential things and he'd given her a stack of loose-leaf watercolour paper that he'd found in the attic.

"Make those cards," he'd encouraged her. "The tourists love them. I'll need to fully restock for the summer season. The added bonus is that I particularly love how it riles that old harpy McShane to know I'm selling them in my shop."

"I don't want to upset her," said Cliona, reluctantly accepting the paper. "She takes my mam's knitting and her scones. She might be an old harpy but it's her business that keeps the wolf from the door."

"Never mind that," Feargus had said, touching a finger to the side of his nose and giving her a conspiratorial wink. "Let me manage Dorothy. You just get yourself back to your drawing, will you?"

Cliona shrugged, fingers playing over the edges of the paper. She used to enjoy making the little notecards. She'd started by hand-lettering tags for her mother's knitting, drawing little pictures of thistles and hawthorn branches to decorate the edges. When Feargus had seen them in Dorothy's shop, he'd pounced on her in the street one day, demanding she expand her repertoire into notecards. She'd done it for a good while, happy to supplement her meagre income from mending nets and helping out in the tea shop down at the quayside. It had helped to pad her coffers as she saved for school. But then it had started to feel too much like settling in to island life. She'd been spending hours out on the moorland, sketching the various flora and fauna. It had expanded into small, pen and ink landscapes; the old abandoned crofts and the sheep dotting the craggy hillsides. One day, she'd caught herself planning a series of seasonal drawings, not of dresses or blouses, as she ought to have been, but a study of the land through the year and that was when she'd stopped.

In the end, she'd taken the offered paper, sandwiched between two pieces of cardboard wrapped in layers of brown paper and then shoved into an old tartan shopper that Feargus had produced from underneath a stack of seed catalogues. It had been easier just to take the paper than argue with her friend. She was far too drained for further efforts.

Trudging up the hill from the village, she let her mind wander over everything she'd learned from her gran and Mrs. Glenbogie. And now, Feargus. There seemed to be a whole undercurrent to life on Glencarragh of which she'd been blissfully unaware. No, she corrected herself, not unaware, just unquestioning. She'd never questioned the collecting of the sea glass. As a small child, she'd happily accepted the story that she'd be helping to preserve the selkie's magic and thereby their ongoing guardianship. As she grew older, it was simply a habit and if, by some strange measure, it ensured that the people of Glencarragh could additionally enjoy the benefits of the tourist boats, if not the tourists themselves, then it was no great hardship to carry on. Sheep and fish only went so far, as it was said during the lengthy meetings about whether or not to allow the tourist boats to run, and it was her secret hope that Ewan would finally realize that captaining a tourist boat was both safer and more lucrative than trying to outwit the fickle sea in search for a decent catch.

A sharp blast of wind staggered her. She clutched at her bag of paper and allowed herself to be blown a few steps sideways, before resetting herself on course. It was common Glencarragh knowledge that you had to let the wind carry you a wee bit if you wanted to get where you were going. The rain had eased at least, reducing itself to a fine drizzle.

The familiar sight of her family's house came into view. Despite the often inhospitable weather, her mother somehow managed to keep the garden trim and productive and the little fence that surrounded the front had a fresh coat of paint every spring. Even now, with everything else having gone over, a tidy hedge of yew and holly enclosed the garden in a sturdy, green barrier against the punishing wind. A curl of smoke spiraled out of the chimney and Cliona imagined the kitchen fire burning brightly and the smell of bread, fresh from the oven. Her da would be down at the pub by now, arguing about tide charts with his cronies. Most of the other fisherman held the official tide charts in light regard, knowing as they did that Glencarragh's tides had a law of their own but Donal insisted they could be relied upon. It was only Ewan's diplomatic interventions that stopped the good-natured bantering from turning into full on brawls.

*Perfect*, she thought, walking around to the kitchen door. *Peace and quiet.*

"Hello!" she called from the utility room which stood just inside the kitchen door. "Is the kettle on?"

She peeled off her sodden mackintosh and hung it on the peg, letting it drip onto the rubber mat beneath. The bag of paper was shoved, unceremoniously, onto a shelf that usually held spare jam jars. Shaking out her wet hair, she made her way into the kitchen, visions of a wedge of warm, fresh-out-of-the-oven bread slathered in blackberry jam in her mind's eye.

A sea of worried faces wasn't at all what she expected. She felt her heart drop and a cold hand clutched at her stomach. A gathering of worried faces in a fisherman's home was never a good thing. With great relief, though, she saw Ewan's face as she scanned the group for clues.

Her mam stepped forward, holding out her hands.

"Come in, pet. The kettle's just on the boil. It's your gran, she's taken a bad turn."

# Chapter 8

"The doctor's in the sitting room with her," said Ewan, patting the empty seat beside him. Cliona, stunned to silence, crossed the floor to sit down.

"What happened?" she said, chewing her lip. "She's alright, isn't she? I just saw her. She was right as rain, feisty as ever."

Ewan put an arm around her shoulder and gave her a squeeze.

"Aye, she'll be fine, I'm sure of it. It's just one of her spells, I expect. But the doctor said she should be somewhere someone can keep an eye on her so Jimmy and me brought her up here."

Cliona nodded at the burly fisherman who sat, somewhat awkwardly, at the head of the table. Their father was nowhere to be seen.

"Where's da? Down at the pub?"

Her tone betrayed a rise of irritation. Now that she knew her gran was going to be okay, she felt the worry turning into anger. Why wasn't he there to look after her gran?

"No, he's not," said Ewan, frowning at her. "He's gone down to the chemist to pick up a prescription. The doctor says she absolutely *has* to start taking her heart medicine."

Cliona swallowed, refusing to feel ashamed for her error. Her da had a history, after all, of serving himself over other people.

"Well, good luck to him, then," she replied, "You know how gran feels about that heart medicine."

"Aye, but I think maybe this time she'll see sense," said Ewan, passing her a steaming mug of tea and shoving the sugar bowl and milk jug along the table. "I think this time she had a bit of a scare."

"Was it that bad?" asked Cliona, the worry returning. She glanced towards the sitting room door. For the second time in a short while, it had become a convalescent room.

"Bad enough," said Helen, coming to join them at the table. She brought a plate, piled high with sausage rolls and cheese scones. Cliona thought of her doorstep of fresh bread and then realized she couldn't possibly eat anything.

"How long will she have to stay?"

"As long as she needs. In fact, I think your da wants to try and convince her to move in with us permanently. He doesn't want her in that drafty little cottage by herself."

"That'll be the day," snorted Cliona, imagining how that conversation would go. "Gran won't ever leave that cottage. She won't give up her independence, you know that."

Her mam nodded, smiling.

"Aye, I know. But your da is worried sick about her and he's as bull-headed as she is."

"Bit of a family trait, that," murmured Ewan, glancing sideways at Cliona then quickly away when she caught him.

"Anyway," continued Helen, "It's enough that she's here for now and we can keep an eye on her for the next couple of days. The doctor says if we can hang onto her for a week, he'll be happy."

Just then, the sitting room door opened, and the doctor walked out, rubbing a hand over his face.

"He must dread having to deal with our gran," said Ewan, under his breath to his sister. "It takes years off the poor man."

Cliona smiled, knowing it was true. The doctor was young, sent to Glencarragh on some scheme to try and bring better medicine to remote areas. He'd been there a couple of years and the strain was starting to show.

"He'll be counting the days 'til his sentence is up," she said. "Must be getting close now."

"I bet he's crossing them off his calendar," agreed Ewan, with a chuckle.

Helen had got up and walked over to the doctor who was pointing to something on the sheet of paper he held. Cliona took advantage of their distraction to slide past and into the sitting room where she found Mrs. Glenbogie sitting beside the settee, her head bowed, and her hands folded on her lap. The old woman looked up when she heard the door open.

"Oh, thank goodness it's you, lass," she said, her face wreathed in a relieved smile. "I thought it was that young upstart again. I don't know what sort of things they're teaching these days at those medical schools, but common sense certainly doesn't seem to be one of them."

Cliona forced a smile. Her eyes were on her gran who was buried under a pile of quilted eiderdowns. The fire was blazing away, and the room felt close and warm.

"The doctor said she has to be kept warm," explained Eileen, seeing Cliona glance at the fire. "Which I can understand. But what I can't fathom is why he says she can't have a window open. A body needs the fresh air if they're to heal. My mother knew that, and so did her mother before her."

She glanced down at her old friend, who appeared to be dozing.

"She'll not be happy to think she's got to be cooped up in a stuffy room. The first thing she'll ask for when she wakes up is that someone open a window. What'll I tell her? It doesn't seem right that she gets herself worked up and that's exactly what she'll do if she can't have a window…"

Eileen Glenbogie's voice cracked and her dark eyes filled with tears. Cliona rushed over to kneel beside her, taking her knobbled hands in her own.

"If Gran wants a window open, then we'll open the bloody window," she said, smiling through her own threatening tears. "As long as herself is kept warm, I can't see why a bit of fresh air should harm. That doctor just doesn't understand that we islanders were born into wind and rain, it doesn't affect us the same as mainland folk. They're just soft, that's all."

Cliona squeezed Eileen's hands. The elderly woman blinked and offered a smile.

"Aye, you're right there, pet. That makes me feel a bit better." She sniffed and cleared her throat.

"Listen," said Cliona, "why don't you go and get yourself a cup of tea and a sausage roll." She squeezed Eileen's hands again when she saw the protest rising on her lips. "I'll sit with Gran until you get back. Go on, give yourself a break. And don't worry, I'll look after her."

Mrs. Glenbogie smiled, grateful for the excuse to stand and stretch her weary limbs. She hadn't realized how she'd been sitting, so hunched and tense as the doctor had examined her dearest friend. She knew now, with a sudden finality and without having to be told, that things weren't ever going to be quite the same again.

"Alright, lass. I will and thank you. I could use a stretch of the old bones as well as a strong up of your mam's tea."

She looked fondly at the peaceful face of her friend, swaddled comfortably under blankets as she dozed in the firelight.

"She's in good hands with you, lass. I haven't a worry in the world."

She patted Cliona on the shoulder and shuffled stiffly out of the room.

Cliona let herself cry then. Slow, silent tears coursed down her cheeks. Fear, relief, frustration; it was all mixed in together. The events of the past few days, along with the strain of the increasing headaches over the previous weeks tumbled over one another in an effort to be the most upsetting. And now this.

She stared at the familiar, beloved face. Relaxed in sleep, Morag's lines and wrinkles smoothed and her mouth curved into a small smile. Stray wisps of white hair stuck out from her usual, tidy bun like dandelion fluff. Cliona felt an aching stab in her chest, the enormity of the love she had for her gran leaving her breathless. To think she would be lost to them some day was a pain she didn't think she could bear. In the way of small children, she'd always thought her gran to be ageless and invincible and she was realizing that she'd never really let go of *that* belief either. She realized that she still considered her gran to be timeless, assuming she'd be with them for always, mostly because that belief had never been challenged. Until now, when she saw, with dawning terror, just how much her gran had aged in the past few years. Eileen, too, although she was two years younger than Morag, seemed to be slowing down.

Cliona swallowed hard, pushing away the implications of those thoughts. She sniffed loudly and rummaged in the pocket of her dress for a hanky.

"Aye, that's a grand idea. Mop up those tears and blow that

nose. You're a soppy mess, you are."

Morag smiled, weakly, from her nest of eiderdowns. She extracted a thin arm and reached out to pat Cliona's knee.

"Go on, give it a good blow. I'll not have you blubbering on these clean blankets."

Cliona smiled and cried and blew her nose. Once she was mopped up and had stuffed the soggy hanky back into her pocket, she leaned over and pressed her cheek against her gran's. Morag's skin was warm and papery. Cliona breathed in the scent of her; a mixture of wind and herbs and the salt of the sea.

"You frightened us, you terrible woman," she whispered, closing her eyes tightly against more tears. She would not cry. "Why must you be so stubborn?"

"If I weren't so stubborn, I'd have shuffled off long ago, my girl," came the sharp reply.

Cliona chuckled, wanting to avoid an argument. She'd leave the tussle over heart medication to more worthy opponents.

Sitting up, she smoothed a hand through her hair. She must look a sight.

"Aye," said her gran, eyeing her with a wicked glint. "You do look a bit like something the cat dragged in."

"Through a hedge backwards, even?" replied Cliona, grinning.

"At least twice," came Morag's quick reply, although there was a breathless quality to her voice.

Cliona let the silence fall, allowing her gran time to steady her breathing. The fire spit and crackled in the grate as a gust of wind howled down the chimney, bringing with it a splatter of rain that sizzled and hissed on the flames. All at once, Cliona was deeply grateful that her gran was there, lying on their sofa in the warm sitting room, rather than in her own cottage down near the sea. It really would be safer to keep her close. She opened her mouth to speak but was stayed by her gran doing the same.

"Eileen's going to need your help, lass. There's no way around it. I'm just not going to be able for it, at least not like I should be."

Morag's voice was quiet but intense with meaning. Cliona inhaled sharply, understanding what was being asked, or rather told, and not liking it at all.

She flicked her gaze to her grandmother. Morag had turned her face to the fire, closing her eyes for a moment as she took a heavy, laboured breath.

There was no way she could argue her way out of this, nor, if she was honest with herself, did she want to. All she really wanted in this moment was to protect her gran and if that meant going along with the fool's errand, then that's what she'd do. Just this once.

She let out a sigh and reached out to lightly touch her gran's arm before lifting it and tucking it back under the eiderdown.

"Just you concern yourself with getting better. You know da won't let you out of here until you're on your feet again, so you need to concentrate on that. Let me and Mrs. Glenbogie manage the rest."

Morag nodded slightly, a small smile on her pale face. She took another, steadier breath and closed her eyes, drifting off to sleep.

The door to the sitting room cracked open and Mrs.Glenbogie poked her head in. She smiled at Cliona and held up a plate on which rested a large slice of bread slathered with blackberry jam.

Cliona smiled and nodded, indicating she'd be right there. She looked back at her gran who was dozing peacefully again. She tucked the eiderdowns tightly around the slight form and placed a gentle kiss on her gran's forehead.

Walking to the door, towards her bread and jam, she heard her gran whisper,

"Skelly. Don't forget Skelly. He'll be with you."

# Chapter 9

The voice in her head had been quiet for several days. Cliona harboured a faint hope that the faery creature invading her mind had simply given up and gone away. The wind had abated slightly and the speculation in the tea shop was that the storm had blessedly passed them over. Indeed, there were patches of blue emerging from behind the clouds which still scudded across the sky, and if not for a deeper knowing, the inhabitants of Glencarragh might have convinced themselves that it was true.

Cliona made her way back down to the quayside. She was meeting Iain and the two of them were going to contribute to the community effort of securing the docked boats against the still-probable storm. It had become a fashion of well-heeled mainlanders to keep pleasure boats docked over the winter and pay the residents to keep an eye on them. Iain had built himself quite a bustling trade in the maintaining and caretaking of the pleasure fleets, as he liked to call them. In addition, two of the resident fishermen were away on the mainland working for the winter and old Hamish Scott was down with bronchitis again. It was an unspoken agreement that folk simply stepped in where others were not able.

The boats were docked in the innermost area of Selkie Bay,

in a naturally occurring cove that had, in a time beyond current memory, been further fortified with a series of large sea walls, built in such a way as to deflect and redirect the force of sea and wind. It was a curious design, much discussed in maritime and engineering circles, as well as being the focus of an archaeological investigation at one point. In addition to providing excellent shelter, the arrangement had the added benefit, Iain had observed, of slowing the tourists down. The high-powered pleasure boats had to chug along at a snail's pace to navigate the labyrinthine entrance to the cove.

The sight of the brightly painted boats bobbing on the water gave Cliona a feeling of soothing familiarity. Her feelings about her island home were complex and often contradictory, but she always found a measure of solace down at the quayside. The tang of salt and fish, combined with an undercurrent of engines and fuel were as welcome to her as the scent of heather up on the moor or the pungent, earthy tones of freshly cut peat.

"Over here!"

Cliona turned her gaze towards the sound of the voice. Iain's mop of black hair was just visible over a pile of yet-to-be-mended fishing nets. He was throwing another rope over the pile and anchoring it to one of the solid posts set into the craggy stone of the pier. There was a series of these posts all along the pier and they were used to anchor everything from boats to bicycles and once, according to island legend, the extensive luggage of a visiting Rajah.

"The lads are worried if the sea breaches the wall, it'll wash this lot away. We haven't time to put them back where they belong so we might as well try and anchor them to the shore," explained Iain, as he criss-crossed the pile again, threading the anchor rope between the layers of nets.

Cliona nodded, and wordlessly set to helping him. It wasn't the first time she'd helped to secure against a storm, after all, not all the storms on Glencarragh were of faery origin, but it was the first time she'd actually been worried about it.

They finished the task in silence then moved on to one of the pleasure boats. Iain checked that the hatches were securely fastened and added several more ropes, pulling the boat up closer against the jetty, rather than letting it swing quite so freely.

"What we need," he said, breath coming in huffing bursts as he hauled on the heavy, oily ropes, "is for these toffs to build us a big dry-dock shed. That would save us a world of trouble every time one of these sodding storms comes."

He glanced over at Cliona, whose face was pinched and pale. She was uncharacteristically quiet and preoccupied.

"Of course, if you could charm your friend into getting rid of them altogether, we wouldn't have to worry about it at all, would we?"

When he got no response, he added,

"Can you pass me the left-handed rope stretcher?"

Cliona blinked, startled from her thoughts by the question. "The what?"

She saw the grin on Iain's face and threw an empty bait bucket at him. He ducked, laughing.

"You were miles away," he said, tying the last knot. "Everything alright? Your gran's back home, so I hear."

Cliona sighed, nodding.

"Yeah, she slept for a couple of days then woke up early and took herself back off home before anyone else was up."

Iain's laugh rang out again.

"Aye, that sounds like our Morag, alright. Good on her. She's a tough old bird."

Cliona smiled.

"She is, that."

"So, what's your bother then?"

Cliona waved a hand, trying to dismiss his concern.

"Nothing important," she said. "Just Ewan and my da are fighting again and then the worry with gran. I'm just feeling a bit low, that's all."

"Is that all?" Iain's face creased into a frown. "Your wee man isn't giving you headaches again, is he?"

She shook her head.

"No, the headaches seem to have gone, thank goodness. I'm just…"

Seeing her face twist into a grimace, Iain climbed out of the boat and held out his hand. She took it and climbed up beside him.

"Tell you what," he said, glancing at the sky. "Let's pop over to the tour shed and have a bit of a break. I've been at this for ages, while you were no doubt lounging about in bed 'til all hours."

He grinned, eyes twinkling with mischief as he saw he'd got a reaction. Cliona opened her mouth to retort but he continued.

"I've got a flask of tea and mam packed me enough sandwiches to feed the entire village. There's not a lot left to do, and I think the rain'll hold off long enough for us to fortify ourselves."

Cliona nodded, grateful for the chance to get out of the wind. Despite her layers of clothing, it seemed to be creeping right into her bones. A hot cup of tea would go down well.

\* \* \*

"So," said Iain, handing her an enamel mug. She clutched it tightly in her frozen fingers, watching the steam wreath into a dancing spiral. "What's really bothering you? Your gran is on the mend, so I can't think of anything else that could have you so tied up in knots."

Cliona shivered and shuffled her stool closer to the little pellet stove that Iain was currently coaxing into life. The tour company's boat shed was far more nicely appointed than most of the fishing sheds. It was more of an office, really, as evidenced by the sleek modern desk and filing cabinet. Detailed maps of the Glencarragh coastline were tacked to the wall, and last summer's tide charts were still spread out on a large table. It also had actual chairs, rather than just overturned beer crates, pilfered from out behind the pub.

She took a tentative sip of her tea, wincing at the heat of it but wanting the scalding liquid to chase away the cold.

After a minute, she spoke.

"I feel like I'm being forced into making a choice," she said, eyes focused on her booted feet. "This whole business with Skelly and the wind singing and the storm," she waved a hand vaguely towards the shed door.

"How do you mean, a choice?" asked Iain. "I thought you already told your gran you'd do your bit?"

"I did," said Cliona, hurriedly. "I'm not backing out. But what will it mean, Iain? Am I then committed to being part of this for always? Because I don't want to be. I don't want to shackle myself to this place. I have other things I want to do."

Iain stiffened, leaning back slightly.

"And is that something to be avoided, then? Being shackled, as you put it, to the island? Is it really so bad to be here?"

Cliona looked up, seeing the hurt flicker across her friend's features.

"No, no. I don't mean it like that. It's just…oh, I don't know how to explain it. Please don't get all defensive with me."

"I don't know how I couldn't," said Iain, his voice clipped. "You're basically suggesting that anyone living here must only be doing so against their will."

"I'm suggesting no such thing," replied Cliona, hotly. "You're being overly sensitive."

"Oh, now I'm too sensitive? Jesus, Clee. What on earth are you thinking? Do you think that just because you have these grand aspirations of traveling the world and other folk are content to live their life here that we're missing out? Because I can tell you, *I* most certainly am not. And neither, I don't doubt, is anyone else you might ask."

Cliona felt the familiar heat of temper rising. Her scalp prickled and her heart thudded painfully. But as quick as it rose, her anger subsided, leaving in its wake a deep fatigue and overwhelming urge to burst into tears.

"I'm not saying that, Iain," she said, her voice wobbling slightly. "I'm not saying that at all."

"Then what *are* you saying?" he asked, softer this time. "Because all I'm hearing is that you're feeling put out by the fact you might have an important role to play here. And that, if I know you at all, is really what's upsetting you."

Cliona lifted her eyes to look at her friend. He leaned towards her, dark eyes reflecting the flickering flames.

"You're upset, Cliona Stewart, because you thought you could get away from here, but now it looks like you can't."

\* \* \*

"You're a direct descendant, you see," explained Eileen.

The dishes had been washed and the kitchen tidied and now the three women sat in the tattered, but comfortable chairs around the fire in the sitting room portion of the open-plan cottage. The rain thrummed steadily against the windows and the wind screamed like a *bean sidhe* through the gap under the kitchen door.

"The first one was born a long, long time ago, nobody really remembers when it was. Time…"

"Moves differently on Glencarragh," finished Cliona, rolling her eyes. "Yes, I've heard the stories. Not that it helps anyone in a practical way. You'd think if we had the gift of faery time, we'd all be looking glamorous into our nineties."

She gave a pointed look to the two women sitting around the fire and at the same time, they all burst into laughter. It was a welcome respite from the tension and seriousness that the conversation had held for what seemed like hours. Cliona glanced at the clock. It *had* been hours.

The laughter died away and the three sat staring into the flickering flames. The warm, earthiness of the peat fire filled the small cottage with comfort and memory. The peat held ancient knowledge, her gran had told her once, as they'd stacked the thick clumps of earth against the wall of the cottage.

"It preserves things," she'd said, "And not just bodies," she added, knowing exactly where fourteen-year-old Cliona would go with that thought. "It preserves the stories of the land. Which is why, when folk gather around a peat fire, the storytelling starts. They can't help themselves, it comes to them in the air, like."

Cliona had dismissed it then, as just another of her gran's stories but in the years to come, having witnessed various family and social gatherings on the island that inevitably ended up around a peat fire, she'd come to see an element of truth in it. When she'd made the observation aloud to Ewan, he'd just shaken his head. "Load of bollocks, that," he'd said. "Folk have been telling stories around fires since the cave men times. It doesn't have to be peat. It's just another one of our gran's tall tales. Faery stories for children."

Cliona had been stung by his response, but instead of making her disbelieve the story, it had only made her hold more firmly to it. The stubborn streak ran in all directions through the Stewart clan.

"So," she said, pulling herself away from the memory. The two old women had started to look dozy. Full bellies and the warmth of the fire was lulling them into a post-prandial nap. She just wanted to get to the bottom of it all.

"I'm a direct descendant of the first wind singer, is that it? And it travels down the female line? Am I getting this?"

Morag blinked, sleepily and smiled over at Eileen who nodded.

"Aye, pet. Just as I am and my own mother before that and so on, down the line."

"Are there others of us? It stands to reason that this first one might have had more than one daughter of her own to go forth and multiply."

Morag shifted uncomfortably in her chair, exchanging a furtive glance with Mrs. Glenbogie.

"We're not quite sure of that, actually. I mean, of course it's possible and record keeping being what it was back then...."

Her voice trailed off and she looked at Cliona, her eyes filled with what looked like worry. Or perhaps it was pity. Cliona couldn't tell.

She gritted her teeth.

"Right, so what you're saying is I'm probably it, then? Other than you, Gran."

Morag nodded.

Cliona turned to Mrs.Glenbogie.

"What about you, then? What's your part in this? I assumed you were one of them as well."

"Us," said Morag, gently. "One of us."

Cliona ignored the correction and remained with her attention on Mrs.Glenbogie.

More glances were exchanged. Cliona let out an impatient sigh.

"Eileen isn't a wind singer, but she's something just as important," said Morag, reaching over to rub her friend's arm. Eileen smiled at her.

"Every wind singer needs an anchor; someone, or something, that will hold them to the earth. You have to understand, lass, singing the wind isn't an easy thing at all. It's meddling with the wild magic and that's not something to be taken lightly. It'll whisk you away as quick as you like. It's no tame creature to be bent to your will."

Cliona swallowed, feeling her mouth become dry. As much as she wanted to dismiss this whole thing as utterly ridiculous, having been brought up hearing stories of faeries and magic meant that belief in the improbable was woven tightly into the fabric of who she was. She was starting to realize the enormity of what was being told to her.

"And Mrs.Glenbogie is your anchor?"

Eileen nodded.

"There's more than a few of us on this island who've been touched by the faery magic in one way or another. In families that have been here for centuries, there's no way around it. Time was, we lived close by with the fae and it all got mingled in. I have a sensitivity to certain things and that's how your gran and I first met. We were both collecting the sea glass, you see?"

The two women grinned at one another, relishing the memory of their girlhood, so long ago.

"And the sea glass we collect *is* selkie glass and you, *we*," Cliona glanced at her gran and Eileen who nodded, encouragingly, "we do indeed collect it to safeguard the selkies. So that they can return safely to the sea, no matter what happens to them on land, and in return they offer guardianship of the island," she finished, smiling, despite herself. She felt like a little girl learning something by rote. The two women had shared their information in such a garbled, cryptic way that it had taken a long time to untangle the basic facts. That was a symptom of spending so long in the company of faeries, she'd mused at one point in the long, meandering conversation, they'd forgotten how to tell a story in a straight line.

"There you are then," said Eileen, with something of a sense of finality. "You've got the idea of it."

The two elderly women grinned at each other, dentures gleaming white in the firelight. No doubt congratulating themselves, thought Cliona, grimly.

"But why?" she persisted, refusing to let the matter go quite yet. "*Why* are there wind singers?"

Morag frowned.

"To sing the wind, of course," she tilted her head sideways and gave Cliona a questioning look, as if wondering if her granddaughter really was that thick. "We can't push back the storms if we don't have the wind."

83

Cliona suppressed a growl of frustration.

"I know that, Gran," she said, fingers gripping handfuls of her skirt as she spoke. "What I need to know is why the whole thing started in the first place," she held up a hand. "I know, I know, the whole lord of the sea arguing with the god of the forest causing the whole big breakdown of life-as-we-know it. Not that. Because that's just the sugar-coated, storied version," she leaned towards the two women who found themselves shrinking against the backs of their chairs in the face of her glare. "What I want to know, is *why* wind singing? Why not just have your friend Skelly magic up something to knock the storms back? Why should *we* have to get involved with faery politics? Because that's what this is, isn't it? Glencarragh is stuck in the middle of some ancient pissing contest between the faeries."

She looked from one dear, lined face to the next, noticing their confusion and feeling her heart sink. It was just so much a part of their way of life that they'd never questioned it. It was perfectly acceptable to them that their lives had been commandeered by this outside force and they were happy to go along with it.

"I just want to know why this is stealing my life."

\* \* \*

Iain snorted with laughter.

"That was a wee bit melodramatic, wasn't it?" he said, tilting his chair back on two legs. "'Stealing your life', is it now?"

Cliona blushed. Perhaps it had been a bit of a melodramatic statement, but it was how she'd felt at the time. No-one seemed to understand how much this was affecting her. It

84

was threatening everything she'd planned. All of her working and saving, all of her careful plotting of how things would go - the internship in Paris, then off to see the world, taking jobs in the most prestigious design houses along the way. Eventually, she conceded, once she'd seen and learned enough, she'd want to settle down somewhere. But that somewhere, in her mind's eye, did not look like Glencarragh.

"It's how I felt," she said, keeping her voice steady. She'd been far more emotional than she preferred, these last few days, feeling herself swinging wildly from despair to acceptance to anger and back to despair, often within a matter of minutes. She was seriously considering the idea that maybe she *was* having a mental breakdown after all. That perhaps this whole thing was just one complicated delusion. But at least the voice in her head had stopped, for now, anyway.

Iain made no comment. Instead, he frowned down at his boots, lips pursed.

Eventually he spoke.

"Would it be such a bad thing," he asked, "to know that you had a place here? Because I know how I'd feel about that."

"Oh? And what's that, then?" Cliona felt her shoulders stiffen, ready for yet another attack. It was so unlike Iain to be combative. She'd hoped for some sympathy but all she'd got so far was argument and accusation.

"I'd be relieved," he said, avoiding her gaze. "I'd be glad to know that I didn't have to worry that I hadn't more ambition than to want to stay and make my life on Glencarragh. I'd like to know, for absolute certain, that I belong here. I'd like to not have to justify why I'm not leaving, like everyone seems to expect I should. I'd like to know that I could settle into myself, just as I am, and not have to think about folk wondering why

I'm not catching the first ferry away."

Cliona sat, stunned into speechlessness. She looked at her best friend's face, feeling a sudden surge of gratitude for its familiarity. Iain was a constant in her days and had been so since that day at nursery school when he offered to share his pot of glue when hers had been stolen by another child. He was confident and bold, always ready to take on a new venture. He was quick to put himself forward to help; always the first one to turn up if something needed building or clearing or tearing down. She hadn't realized that much of that was a part of his need to find a way to belong on the island. And all of this time, she'd been fighting her own belonging, tooth and nail.

"I'm sorry, Iain," she said, softly. "I had no idea."

"Aye, well. You wouldn't, would you?" he said, his tone light but his eyes filled with sadness. "You always were so taken with your own self and your own struggles."

Cliona knew he was joking, and also that he wasn't. She felt a stab of guilt and shame. Suddenly she wanted to make everything right for him, to let him know how much he meant and how much he belonged. She'd been neglectful too long of that. She leaned over and took one of his hands in hers. The skin was rough and calloused. Fisherman's hands, an islander's hands. Whatever he thought of himself, whatever his doubts, his hands told the truth of who he was.

"Will you be my anchor?" she asked, "I'm going to need a good one. Lord knows I haven't a clue what I'm doing, and I can't think of anyone I'd want more to keep me to the earth than you. You're the only person I can imagine who has the strength to hold me to this place."

The young man's face was impassive. His dark eyes reflected the light flickering from the pellet stove and his mouth was set in a straight line. But she saw him swallow and blink several times before, in a voice that was raw with emotion, he said,

"Aye, I reckon I could do that for you, for Glencarragh."

# Chapter 10

"Along time ago, on Glencarragh," began Morag, her eyes focused steadily on the flickering of the fire, "the islanders had a different way of keeping the storms under control. Now, back then, they were more your garden-variety storms, nothing like what we have now. But to those simple folk, they were fearsome enough. They didn't have the boats we have, nor the weather forecasts and radios and satellites and all that which makes it a bit safer out on the water,"

"Such as you ever are," added Mrs. Glenbogie, sagely.

Morag nodded to her friend, "Aye, indeed."

She paused a moment and the two women seemed lost in thought. Cliona bit back a sigh of frustration.

"Anyway," continued Morag, resettling herself in her chair. "As I said, it was a different time and a different way of doing things; it was a desperately hard life and the folk lived always on the edge of existence, trying to scrape a living from the moor and the sea."

Cliona felt Skelly's presence in her mind; there were no words, only a stirring. She closed her eyes and concentrated, willing him to go away. A jab of pain flashed across her skull and she let out a small gasp.

"Don't fight him, lass," said Eileen, her voice soft and soothing. "The pain will ease if you stop fighting."

Cliona grunted, opening her eyes. She focused on her breathing, trying to relax. The stirring stopped and she felt his presence dissipate slightly. But he was still there, like movement caught at the corner of her eye.

"The story goes, that after one too many seasons of terrible storms, of great loss to life and property, the folk struck a bargain with the faery people. There was one, and you'll recognize the name, Lira, who was summoned, and the terms were cast and agreed upon."

"Mind, there's some that say those storms weren't natural after all," said Mrs. Glenbogie, stepping into the telling as Morag sat back in her chair, silently sipping her tea. "That it was Lira herself had brought the despair upon the island in the first place, to force the people into coming to her."

"Why would she do that?" asked Cliona. "I thought her lot didn't want anything to do with mortals. Isn't that why Skelly got booted out in the first place? It doesn't follow that she'd want to get involved with humanity."

"If there's one thing you can learn about the faery folk," said Eileen, with a rueful smile, "it's that they've got very long memories. Not only that, they've the patience that comes from having centuries to bide their time."

A soft chuckle came from Morag's chair. She had lain her head back against the wings of the chair, a smile playing across her lips.

She looks tired, thought Cliona, worrying. This has all been too much.

"So?" she asked, wanting to move things along.

"So," said Eileen, with an apologetic shrug. "No-one seems to know for certain. It's a thread of the tale that got lost along the way. Mebbe she took it into her head that exiling Skelly and his people wasn't sufficient revenge. Perhaps she decided she wanted to make the land-walkers suffer too. Nobody knows, really. It's not as if they're in the habit of explaining themselves. The point is, she's a nasty piece and she struck a vile bargain with the poor, suffering folk of Glencarragh, that affected the lives of the young women of the island for generations."

Cliona frowned, casting her mind back through the stories she'd heard at her gran's knee. Her father hadn't wanted Morag to tell his daughter the old tales, but her gran had done so anyway, filling the young girl's mind with the history and legends of the island. Young Cliona had absorbed it like a sponge, fascinated and entranced. She remembered a very old one, one that seemed a bit too far-fetched that it couldn't possibly be real.

"The sea brides," she murmured, a shiver passing over her.

The two old women nodded, almost simultaneously and all three of them sat in thoughtful silence for a few moments.

The fire popped and hissed. A gust of wind screeched down the chimney making the flames dance wildly. Cliona shivered again, pulling her cardigan more tightly around her.

"Aye," said Morag, her voice lilting gently, "those were dark days on Glencarragh. Dark days indeed."

She cleared her throat noisily, breaking the reverent silence.

"Anyway, it came to pass that the folk of Glencarragh had an ally among the faery people, and no," she held up a hand as Cliona opened her mouth to speak, "not who you might think, although your one Skelly could be in that number I suppose. No, this is a creature far older and far more powerful. Cernach, is what he calls himself."

She paused again, as if collecting her thoughts. Mrs. Glenbogie leaned towards her slightly, then sat back as Morag gave a tiny shake of her head.

"It's been said that this fellow decided to step in and do something to thwart Lira and her terrible goings-on. He had, no doubt, an agenda of his own, but all that mattered was that he was able to intervene."

"And so, to make a long story very short," said Mrs.Glenbogie, ignoring the look of tired protest on Morag's face. "his interference resulted in the first wind singer."

Cliona blinked at the sudden switch from her gran's leisurely storytelling to Mrs. Glenbogie's abrupt summation. She looked at her gran and saw the weariness etched in her face, then to Eileen who gave her a pointed glance.

Sighing, she nodded.

"I see," she said, "so a faery intervening in another faery's dealings with mortals produced the wind singer line."

"Right you are, lass. They have some very definite rules of engagement, that lot, but somehow, always seem to manage to get around them in all sorts of tricksy ways."

"They're manipulative bastards, you mean," said Cliona, dryly. It had been many years since she'd been charmed by the idea of the faery folk. There was, as far as she could see, nothing romantic or delightful about them and recent events only proved that line of thinking.

Morag tutted, shaking her head at Cliona's language but Eileen simply grinned.

"Well, it's true, Gran," said Cliona, her voice clipped and bitter. "They're still using us, aren't they? Even though they pretend they've done us a grand favour, giving us the ability to manage the storms. We're just their playthings, no matter how you try and dress it up with noble callings or whatever bollocky mess this is."

"That's enough, Cliona," warned Eileen, shooting a worried glance at Morag who seemed to have shrunk into her chair. "Maybe you need to be thinking less of yourself in all of this, less of how it's affecting you and more about how it's affecting your gran."

Cliona blushed, guilt washing over her in a familiar wave. It was true. In her own temper and righteous indignation, she was, yet again, dismissing how everyone else was feeling.

"I'm sorry, Gran," she said, getting up to go to her grandmother's chair. She kneeled down and took hold of the old woman's hands. "I'm a selfish beast, I know. This is has just all been so sudden. I suppose I'm having a hard time getting my head around it all. Please don't be cross with me. I'm trying, I really am."

Her gran smiled, taking back a hand so she could smooth it over Cliona's red curls.

"It's alright, pet," she said, her voice hoarse. "We didn't handle this at all well. It's been hard, what with your da taking so against anything that isn't a tide chart or a weather forecast. He's made it difficult for me to do my duty by you. But that's not a fit excuse. I could have found a better way."

"No, Gran!" exclaimed Cliona, anxious to comfort her beloved grandmother. "Don't blame yourself, not ever. And da might be pig-headed and difficult but, let's face it, so am I."

The two older women exchanged an amused look.

"I've not made this easy for either of you, and I'm sorry. Look, let me have a few days to sort it all out in my head. I promise not to cause any more trouble with it."

She was close to tears. Blinking furiously and swallowing

the hard clog that was burning in her throat. She leaned over and gave her gran a gentle but firm hug, burrowing her face into the familiar smells of peat-smoke and salt and heather.

Her gran rubbed one hand up and down her back, soothing and calming, while the other returned the hug. Mrs. Glenbogie patted her shoulder.

"There now, pet," she said, her sing-song voice as familiar to her as when she was a small girl upset over a skinned knee or a missed piece of selkie glass. "It's going to be alright in the end, you'll see. You've a long line of women holding you as sure as your gran is holding you now. And there's a powerful magic in that."

# Chapter 11

*Y*ou've got it sorted, then?

Skelly's voice echoed in her mind. It wasn't as startling as it once was, but she couldn't help but jump slightly at the sudden invasion of her silent thoughts.

*What do you mean?* she sent back, fully knowing the answer but unable to stop her contrary impulse; that one was a losing battle.

*You've come to a peace with it all?*

When Cliona didn't answer, the faery added, *I've let you alone, as you've probably noticed.*

Cliona grunted aloud, then glanced quickly around her. The street was deserted; the weather was too foul now for even the hardiest of village shoppers. Having left Iain at the tour boat shed, she was making her way towards her gran's cottage. The wind and rain made it difficult going.

*I don't know if I have a peace with it,* she eventually replied. *But my gran isn't well, and I understand that she'll need my help with managing this storm. After that, well, I can't promise anything.*

A bark of hollow laughter echoed in her head.

*This isn't a one-off thing, lassie. This is your birthright and you don't have the luxury of choosing your fancy.*

Cliona gritted her teeth against a rising tide of frustration.

94

Deep down she knew he was right; she simply wasn't ready to believe it had to be true.

A sensation of unexpected sorrow washed suddenly over her. She inhaled a sharp gasp, as the weight of it lodged heavily in her chest. Images flickered through her mind; leaden skies and banks of black, cloud. The sea roiled and foamed, crashing thunderously against the shore, waves breaking over the sea walls as the storm advanced towards Glencarragh. Her mind's eye caught sight of flickering movement under the surface of the sea; flashes of long-limbed figures, pale against the black sea, astride dark horse-shaped creatures with gaping, sharp-toothed mouths.

Cliona put a hand to her head as a particularly strong blast of wind knocked her sideways. She steadied herself against a lamppost, trying to blink away the images in her mind.

*What are you doing?* she whispered, frightened and angry. *Stop it. I won't let you frighten me.*

The same hollow laugh echoed in her thoughts. *I'm not trying to frighten you. What you see is what has been and what yet will be. If it scares you, then that should tell you all you need to know.*

*Leave me alone,* she said, *this isn't fair.*

*No,* said Skelly, *I don't suppose it is, lass. I don't suppose it is at all.*

Cliona felt a momentary pang of shame, before shoving it firmly away. What had happened to Skelly was his own doing, she reminded herself. He had made his choices and now he was dealing with the consequences. He had no right to put that on her or anyone else.

With those bolstering thoughts and a great effort of will, she closed her mind to the invading faery, accepting the ripple of pain in her head as she did so.

A few more minutes of battling the buffeting wind and she arrived at her gran's cottage. She was pleased to see a curl of smoke coming from the chimney and a glow of light in the window. Gran must be up and about.

She knocked on the blue painted door and called out as she walked in.

"Hallooo! Anyone home?"

"In here, pet," came the reply.

Frowning, Cliona walked down the passage and pushed open the door to the kitchen. It had been Mrs.Glenbogie's voice that had answered her.

"Where's Gran?" demanded Cliona as she entered the kitchen. She looked around the room and saw no sign. Eileen was standing at the stove, stirring a large pot of something that was sending delicious tendrils of scent into the air. The rumble in Cliona's stomach reminded her she hadn't eaten lunch. The argument with Iain had left her unable to sample any of his mother's sandwiches.

Cliona pushed that away and turned her attention to Mrs.Glenbogie.

"She's just gone for a bit of a rest," said Eileen, avoiding Cliona's gaze. "I think she's been overdoing it. You know how she is."

Mrs. Glenbogie gestured to the large scrubbed pine dresser where row upon row of jars and bottles shone in the light of the lamps.

"She's been putting up her jam and her cordials," she explained. "I told her to wait, that the fruit would keep in the deep freeze for another couple of weeks, but she wouldn't have it. You know how she gets," she said again, as if to apologize. "She said folk would need them, what with the weather having turned and the damp setting in."

Cliona nodded, wordless. Her gran and Mrs.Glenbogie had been the unofficial herb wives of Glencarragh for as long as she could remember. It wasn't anything intentional, simply something they'd fallen into. Gran's elderberry and rosehip cordial was in high demand during the winter months.

"Why didn't she ask for help?" she said, cross with herself for not predicting that this would happen. "I could've done it for her. I know the recipe."

"Aye, and so do I. But you know how she is," said Eileen, repeating herself. She shrugged and waved her ladle towards one of the doors leading off the kitchen.

"She's in her bedroom. To rest her eyes, she said, but I'm guessing she's lying there planning her kitchen garden."

Cliona offered a weak smile.

"Here," said Eileen, walking to the dresser to retrieve a soup mug. "Take her a bit of broth. She could do with some fortification."

Cliona accepted the mug of steaming, fragrant broth. It was another standard on Glencarragh - made from a recipe handed down through generations of island women who were used to treating the ailments of sea and moor. She breathed in the herbed scent, feeling her mouth water.

"When you've finished bullying her into drinking it," said Eileen, smiling, "I'll have a bowl for you out here. With a nice doorstep of my bread, aye?"

Cliona nodded, grateful.

She knocked lightly on the bedroom door then opened it slowly, peering around to make sure her gran wasn't actually asleep. But as Eileen had surmised, the old woman was propped up on her pillow, holding a pad of paper, pencil poised as she looked to see who was entering the room. Her face wreathed in a smile when she saw it was Cliona.

"I thought I heard your voice," she said, putting down her pad and paper to stretch out her arms. "Come and sit, love. You're a sight for weary eyes, that's to be sure."

Cliona walked over to her gran, her heart thudding. The little woman looked smaller still, her tiny frame hardly more than a small child's, buried under a thick eiderdown. She was wearing an old flannel jacket that had belonged to Cliona's grandad, over her thick cotton nightgown. It was like she was shrinking before her eyes.

Setting the soup mug gently on the nightstand, Cliona took her grandmother in her arms for a hug. She swallowed hard, noticing how thin her gran had become. She gave her a quick squeeze and then pulled back, reaching for the broth.

"Now, I'm having no argument," she said, holding out the mug. "Mrs. Glenbogie has made some lovely broth and you look like you haven't been eating properly. It's time you started building yourself up again. Come on, drink up. I'm not leaving until it's all gone."

Morag smiled, her eyes dancing.

"Bossy little madam, aren't you?" she said, accepting the mug. She took a small sip. "Lovely, that."

"Yes, it is. So, drink it down. When was the last time you had a proper meal? Probably when you were at ours."

Her gran shrugged, dutifully taking another sip of broth.

"I haven't had much appetite," she admitted. "And I've been busy getting things in order. But don't worry, your mam has been plying me with meals."

"But are you *eating* them?" asked Cliona. "They're not much good to you if you leave them sitting in the fridge."

"I have a nibble, here and there," said her gran, waving a bony hand. "Now, enough about me. How are things with you, my lamb?"

Cliona fiddled with a loose thread on the eiderdown.

"Alright, I suppose," she answered, carefully avoiding her gran's eyes.

"And Himself? Is he after pestering you much?"

Cliona snorted.

"We had words earlier, but he's mostly been leaving me alone."

Morag nodded, thoughtful. She set the mug down on the nightstand. Cliona picked it up again and handed it back.

"Drink, or I'll starve to death myself. Mrs.Glenbogie said I can't have mine until you've drank yours and I'm perishing with hunger."

Her gran let out a bark of laughter and accepted the mug again.

"Well, we can't have that, can we? I'll sup a moment, then we'll have a wee chat, shall we?"

\* \* \*

A half hour later, Cliona emerged from the bedroom. A large bowl of broth sat, steaming on the kitchen table, accompanied by a several thick slices of freshly buttered bread. A buxom, flowered teapot stood on a trivet next to the bowl, along with a mug, sugar bowl and bottle of milk.

"Sit yourself down, pet," said Mrs.Glenbogie, taking the empty mug from her hands. "You look done in."

Cliona slid into a chair, propping her head up with her hands for a moment before speaking.

"Is she going to be alright? I mean, really, not just what you think I want to hear."

Eileen sighed.

"I honestly don't know, love," she said, glancing towards the bedroom door. "She's as tough as an old boot, we both know that. But this was a very bad spell with her heart and she's not resting like she should be. What she really needs, is a couple of weeks in one of those convalescent homes or some such, but we both know she won't do that."

Cliona rolled her eyes.

"That'd be the day," she said, smiling for a moment at the thought of her grandmother being wheeled about in a wheelchair or gathering for a singsong in a common room. "Is she at least taking her medicine?"

Eileen nodded.

"Aye, that much she'll agree to."

A sudden crash made them both jump. A gust of wind blasted through the kitchen, sending papers flying from where they'd been sitting on the dresser.

"The door," said Cliona, getting up. "I mustn't have latched it properly."

Sure enough, the front door had blown open. The wind rushed down the passage, bringing dried leaves from the garden in with it. A spattering of rain lashed Cliona's face as she pushed against the door and leaned on it, hard, as she secured the latch. She slid the chain across as well, for good measure.

Returning to the kitchen, she was startled to see the look of worry and fear on Eileen's face. Seeing Cliona's expression, the elderly woman smiled, and shook her head.

"It needs a new latch on it, I think," she said, turning to the sink. "Maybe your Ewan will come and have a look at it. We can't have that happening every time the wind has a bit of a go at it, can we?"

Cliona stood for a moment, watching her old friend busying herself at the sink, filling the deep enamel dish bowl with sudsy water. She felt a sudden and profound realization settling over her. There really was no way around this for her.

"She won't be able to sing the wind at all this time, will she?" she asked, her voice barely above a whisper. "I'm going to have to do this by myself, aren't I?"

The old woman didn't turn around, but Cliona saw her shoulders sag and her head bow.

The wind hurled itself at the cottage, rattling the windowpanes, making Cliona flinch.

"I'm sorry, lass," was all she said. "It wasn't supposed to be like this."

# Chapter 12

The wind pushed and shoved at her as she wound her way down the path towards the sea. Her hair flew in wild tendrils, having escaped from the scarf she'd wrapped around her head as she stood in the shelter of her gran's doorway.

"He'll find you," Mrs.Glenbogie had assured her, handing Cliona a small linen bag. The contents clicked dully together, and Cliona looked sharply up at Eileen.

"Aye, well," the older woman said, "It's as well may be that you'll need to call on the extra magic a bit. Just keep a hold of it, we don't know when the storm will come and no doubt you'll be busy with Himself."

At Cliona's questioning glance she said, "Don't worry, the selkie folk won't take any hurt with it, it's to their benefit as well that we keep that nasty bit under our thumbs, aye?"

Cliona nodded, wordlessly, accepting the bag of sea glass and shoving it into the deep pockets of her mackintosh.

"Let your feet take you where they want to go," continued Mrs. Glenbogie, "and leave your mind and heart open." She paused to squeeze the younger woman's shoulder. "And don't worry about your gran. I'll not leave her 'til I see she's settled with some supper."

102

Cliona nodded again, managing a small smile, before taking a deep breath and stepping out into the wind and rain.

Her feet took her through the village and out to the cliff path, but instead of going up onto the cliff and out to the moor, as she would have expected, she took the right-hand fork and started down to the beach.

As she walked, Cliona mulled over the conversation she'd had with her Gran. It had been a comfort and a terror all at once as Morag had left nothing out concerning the danger of what faced her granddaughter. By tradition and the usual way of things, Cliona ought to have had years to train as a wind singer. Natural inclination, it seemed, wasn't quite enough. Or at least, it wasn't recommended. But Cliona's loud insistence that she was going to go away to school had meant a long delay.

\* \* \*

"But why didn't you tell me how long it would take?" Cliona had wailed, holding her gran's cold hands between her own. "And now you're not well, we can't be having you standing out in the wind and rain teaching me."

Morag had chuckled.

"No, lass. The spirit might be willing, but the flesh? Well, I think the flesh is happier here, tucked in my bed with a nice fire going."

Cliona chafed her gran's hands between hers, trying to rub warmth into them, unwilling to say the words which were echoing around in her mind.

It was all her fault. She'd been selfish and stubborn and only half-serious about the whole mad reality that was her island home. Far away, in the bustle of city life, it had been easy to think of Glencarragh and selkie glass and faery-storms with a sort of detached amusement. It was the stuff of children's tales and hardly relevant when there she was, immersed in art and fashion and everything she'd ever wanted in life.

"You had to have your life, pet," said Morag, as if reading her mind. "It wouldn't have done anyone any good if you'd been denied that, now would it?"

Cliona forced a smile, looking down at the embroidered eiderdown.

"No, I suppose not. I would have fought you tooth and nail. It's just…"

"You have other plans, I know. And believe me, Eileen and I have spent hours arguing over it. I always felt, as did your mam, that we should let you go; let you get on with the life that you want for yourself. We thought that maybe it's time we reckoned with things head-on and not keep putting off the inevitable. But when you came back, when your schooling was finished and there you were, I thought maybe…"

Morag's voice faded away and she stared at the flames flickering and darting in the fireplace.

"Never mind that," she said, leaving the thought unfinished. "The point is, it's far past the time that the women of Glencarragh should cease to be punished for things not of their doing."

Cliona glanced up, eyes wide, at the bitterness in her grandmother's voice.

Morag smiled and squeezed Cliona's hands before removing one and placing it against her granddaughter's cheek.

"Och, listen to me," she said, her pale blue eyes regaining some of their twinkle. "'Tis just the mad mutterings of an old lady. Now, here's what we're going to do. You'll not like it, I know that already, but it's all we have left to us for now. Once I'm up and about, we can get you sorted properly."

\* \* \*

The rasping shout of a gannet pulled her from her thoughts and an accompanying gust of wind forced her to concentrate on her footing. The rickety staircase leading down to the beach was slick with rain and she slipped and slid down the final few steps, clutching at the wobbling bannister, cursing silently as she stepped onto the wet sand.

The sea churned a grey-green, the rolling waves capped with foamy white tips at it frothed onto the shore. A pair of kittiwakes rode the currents of wind, rising and falling almost playfully.

"Lucky sods," muttered Cliona, watching as they tumbled and rose before wheeling away towards the cliffs. Not for the first time, she looked on the birds of Glencarragh with a sort of awed envy. It was a tired metaphor, but it was tired because it resonated so deeply with the very human desire for freedom and escape. She closed her eyes, imagining herself lifting off and leaving all of the worry and trouble behind. She'd never looked on the pigeons of Glasgow with the same envy. That, in itself, told her everything.

"Careful what you wish for, lass. It's a powerful thing, is wishing."

Cliona let out a stifled scream and staggered sideways, turning to look at the wiry old man who had appeared beside her on the sand. His tweed cap, pulled low on his head against the imprecations of the weather, was beaded with moisture from the rain and his battered overcoat billowed and snapped in the wind. Worn corduroys were tucked into large, black wellington boots and he was leaning casually on what looked like a carved shepherd's crook, sunk into the sand. His sharp emerald eyes met hers, twinkling with something like mischief.

"Sorry, did I give you a fright? You ought not to let folk sneak up on you like that."

Cliona swallowed hard, fighting down the urge to run; she'd recognized his voice immediately. He sounded much the same in person as he had done in her head. She put a hand to her temple in an unconscious gesture.

"Aye, lass. That should ease now. Mind, it wouldn't have been so bad if you weren't such a bloody-minded harridan."

Cliona inhaled sharply, turning to face the old man, who stood facing the water, a strange, pinched look on his lined, sun-browned face.

Something in his expression halted the stream of indignation that was about to leave her lips. She remembered what her gran had told her.

"Why are we here, of all places?" she asked, gesturing towards the mutinous sea. "Aren't you in some kind of existential agony for being so close?"

Skelly cleared his throat and turned to face her.

"True," he acquiesced, wincing visibly as the rolling surf crept towards the toes of his boots, "I am that. But I thought it a gesture of goodwill, aye?"

At Cliona's puzzled look, he nodded first towards the sea and then poked a gnarled finger on her streaming mackintosh, in the center of her chest.

"It seems only fair that you see the scope of my penance, so you know that I understand the scope of what you see as yours."

Cliona swallowed, feeling the unwelcome sting of tears prickling behind her eyes. Not only that, there was the distinct and uncomfortable burn of shame rising to flush her cheeks. Her so-called penance was nothing to hundreds of years of exile and the dissolution of one's people. Her shoulders slumped and she felt the anger and indignation draining away. She sighed heavily, turning to glance first at the sea and then back at the shining black of the cliffs.

"Come on, then," she said, pushing a strand of wet hair from her face. "We'd better get you away from here before you collapse in an undignified heap."

Cliona turned her back on the old man and started towards the stairs. When he didn't follow, she turned around.

Skelly stood, leaning heavily now on his stick, his eyes gazing out over the surging waves. His lips moved silently, and his free hand clenched into a fist.

Cliona felt a pang of something that she didn't want to acknowledge and started to make her way back up the slippery stairs.

# Chapter 13

"Again!"

Skelly's stick thudded on the sodden turf, sending up a squelching splat of water. The wind swirled and eddied around the two figures - one crouched, breathing heavily, the other leaning over with a hand gripping the shoulder of his companion.

Iain raised his head to look into the impassive face of the old man, his own face wild with fear and worry.

"She's knackered," he said, raising his voice over the roar of wind and surf. "Give her a minute, won't you?"

The trio stood near the edge of the cliffs, looking out over Glencarragh Bay, or, Selkie Bay as it was named in the tourist brochures. The fishing boats, as tiny as children's toys, bobbed in the distant quayside like a string of corks and smoke curled in thin plumes from the chimneys of the grey stone houses lining the meandering streets. It was a picture postcard view and, indeed, there had been more than a few photographs taken from that very spot and was one of the more popular images to be purchased from Dorothy McShane's gift shop. But those were photographs taken on mild, cloudless days when the sea sparkled with twinkling gemstones of the reflected light of a warming sun. Today, the sky was leaden and the sea a roiling, churning mass of seething blackness as the wind hurled periodic spats of rain at their cold-numbed hands and faces. Skelly leaned casually against a gnarled hawthorn, itself leaning in perpetual acknowledgement of the prevailing wind.

"She won't have the luxury of a minute when the storm rises," replied Skelly, his voice flat and unwavering. He nodded towards Cliona who was struggling to her feet. She shook off Iain's hand and pushed her sodden hair back from her face. She gave Skelly a hard-eyed glare as she worked to steady her breathing.

"See? She's right as rain. Now, both of you, get your heads straight and do it again."

Iain shot the old man a murderous look and moved to stand beside Cliona, his shoulder bracing hers. She flicked a glance at him, and he nodded, taking several deep breaths. He closed his eyes and tried to concentrate.

He'd been told that his job was to simply stand firm; to be an anchoring presence for Cliona as she worked to call and then control the wind. But it was all very vague and abstract and that wasn't how he liked things to be. Engines and tide charts; maneuvering boats through the maze of underwater stone in the harbour, knowing the best times and places to catch glimpses of the seals, chatting up the tourists and knowing who might be difficult and who was easy to please, those were the things he knew. Those were things you could put your hand on, could navigate by, not the strange and elusive ideas in which he was being forced to participate. He'd always known he would walk over hot coals for his best friend, and right now, he was thinking that would be far preferable to what he was being asked.

The first few attempts had been disastrous. Cliona, according to the old man who was, unbelievably, the omnipresent force to whom they all owed their safety, lacked discipline and focus. She was willful and resistant to guidance. Iain had actually snorted with laughter as Skelly had berated his friend, avoiding the angry glares that he knew Cliona would be sending his way. He could have told the old man that. He could also tell him that those exact qualities were what made her resilient and persistent and had lifted her up and out of Glencarragh to pursue her dreams with a single-minded determination that suffered no gainsayers. Those were the qualities that would carry her when everything else rallied against them. The lack of discipline and focus that Skelly observed were simply a result of Cliona having not made up her mind to fully commit to the task at hand. It was that, thought Iain, which should be worrying the old man. Because it was certainly worrying him.

Iain steeled himself for the force of what was coming. He could feel Cliona tense as she gathered herself, sending her focus inward.

* * *

It was, apparently, a matter of simply allowing what was already there to rise to the surface. Skelly had attempted to explain it, but it had made no sense to either of them and in the end, he'd just waved his hand in dismissal and suggested she just try and see what happened. What had happened had shocked them all, even, although he wouldn't admit it, Skelly himself. What could only be described as a miniature tornado had come roaring across the ground, appearing over the horizon, screaming through the heather before disappearing over the edge of the cliff in a flurry of sticks and tufts of grass and even an old, red rubber bucket likely left in one of the stone lambing pens from further across the moor.

Subsequent attempts had resulted in less violent outcomes, although with no further finesse or control.

"What does it bloody matter if it's neat and tidy?" Cliona had shouted in frustration after Skelly's umpteenth lecture on her need to have better control. "Don't I just have to hold it down to a dull roar until it blows itself out? Surely, I've enough space over the open sea for that. No-one's going to bloody well care if I can stuff it into a teacup as long as the boats don't end up in the village hall."

Skelly regarded her, eyes narrowed, his sharp emerald ones meeting Cliona's own, unflinching, green. Iain took an unconscious step back, his gaze going between the red-haired girl and the white-haired man. It was like watching two roosters deciding which one was going to attack first; all circling, chest-puffing show and bluster.

"It matters," said Skelly, finally, through gritted teeth. "It matters and we've no time to be standing here arguing about it, so you'll just have to believe me when I tell you. And if that's too much for your pig-headed brain to manage then there's no point in carrying on. I feel satisfied that I've done my sworn duty and you can just get your foolish self back down the cliff and explain it to yon old ones, aye?"

At that, Cliona had looked away. Iain let out a long breath that he hadn't realized he'd been holding. After that, it had gone more or less without argument.

\* \* \*

"That's it, lass," murmured Skelly, as he watched Cliona settle back her shoulders. Her fingers brushed against Iain's and he planted his booted feet more firmly onto the turf. "*Use* your anchor; he's got all the strength of the island in him and he'll give you the measure of earth you need. Now, let the song rise and...gently now, not too quickly. Steady on...ah, bollocks..."

A roar, like the sound of a speeding freight train deafened them, obliterating all other noise. Iain staggered sideways as the force of the wind pushed between him and Cliona. Skelly shouted something, gesturing wildly but Cliona's eyes were closed, and a strange smile tugged at the corners of her mouth. Another violent gust buffeted Iain, knocking him right off his feet and preventing him from rising. With a sudden wild panic, he realized he was being pushed towards the edge of the cliff. He called to Cliona, trying to catch her attention as he dug his fingers into the earth in a crazed effort to hold himself in place, but his friend was oblivious, arms raised outwards as the wind swirled and danced and roared.

That's it then, thought Iain, as he felt his grip on the earth weakening. He almost laughed, a hysterical cackling laugh, what a bloody ridiculous way to go.

His last memory was of a blur of blue-green skin and the sound of someone crying.

# Chapter 14

"Abso-bloody-lutely *not*!" shouted Cliona, her face white and her hands shaking as she hauled Iain to his feet. His own face was nearly as white as Cliona's and he wobbled slightly as he tried to walk as far back from the cliff edge as he could get. Skelly stood, his arms folded across his chest, his stick tucked into the crook of his elbow. Despite the persistent wind and rain, his tweed cap and overcoat remained dry and unmolested.

"I'm *not* doing that again," repeated Cliona, clutching Iain's elbow as if to hold him onto the earth. "Did you not just see what happened? I almost killed my best friend!"

Her voice rose in a frightened shriek, which alarmed Iain only slightly less than the fact he'd almost been blown over the cliff edge. Cliona never got frightened. At least, she would never admit to it.

"I'm alright, Clee," he said, regaining his voice. "Didn't our man here just save the day…." He paused, trying to remember exactly what had happened but he found himself unable to grasp the images that flitted just out of view of his mind's eye. He cast a sharp look at Skelly who simply stared back, unblinking. Iain looked away. He hadn't quite decided if the old fellow was someone to be trusted; there was something not at all right about him. He shook his head, gently removing

Cliona's clutching fingers from his elbow.

"I don't care," said Cliona, crossing her own arms and jutting out her chin. "This is just too much to ask. You're all expecting me to master something I've supposed to have had years to work on. Well, I won't do it. I won't put anyone else at risk like that."

"And what, lassie, do you think you'll be doing if you *don't* keep at it?"

Skelly's voice was soft, yet despite the wind and roaring surf crashing into the base of the cliffs, they could hear him without effort.

Cliona's eyes grew wary.

"Don't try and guilt me," she said, pushing back her shoulders. "That doesn't work. Besides," she continued, faltering slightly under the weight of the old man's steady gaze. "I never said I was giving up forever. Just for today. I'm tired."

Skelly gave a slight nod of his head, regarding Iain with the same steady, calculating look before turning back to Cliona, his expression unreadable.

"As you like."

And then he was gone.

"What the hell?" said Iain, eyes wide. "Where did he go?" He whirled around, as if expecting the old man to pop out from behind the hawthorn.

"Oh, who cares?" said Cliona, wearily. "I'm just glad the sodding menace is gone. Come on, I'm dying for a cuppa. I bet Feargus has some of those gorgeous cinnamon buns. I'm bloody starving."

She tucked her arm into the crook of Iain's elbow, mustering every last ounce of energy she could draw upon to sound as casual and as matter of fact as possible. She couldn't bear for

Iain to know how deeply terrified she was and how she was still shaking inside from what had very nearly happened on the edge of the cliff. Because it wasn't even so much that she had lost control of the wind; it was that one brief moment when she didn't *want* to control it.

\* \* \*

"Another glorious day in Glencarragh!" said Feargus, beaming as the two bedraggled figures clattered through the door of his shop. "Good heavens!" he added, taking one look at their white faces and rain-soaked hair plastered against their skulls. "What have you two been up to? You look like death warmed over. Come on, up to the flat. I'll put the kettle on."

"Ah, that'd be grand, Feargus," said Iain, his tired face creasing into a grateful smile. "You've no idea how grand."

Feargus watched the pair make their way down the narrow passage to the door that led up to his flat. He saw Iain place a steadying hand on Cliona's lower back as she reached up to unlatch it. His face furrowed into a frown as he crossed the creaking wooden floor to turn the sign over to the side that said "Closed". He peered out of the window at the streaming rain. It was unlikely that anyone would be out today anyway and besides, folk were used to his erratic opening hours and knew to just come back later. He flinched as a sudden gust of wind blasted against the door, rattling the frame and sending the doorbell jingling softly.

"Bollocks," he muttered, closing his eyes briefly, then went to see to the young ones.

115

* * *

"And you say you nearly blew Iain off the cliff?" said Feargus, his eyes wide and his hand pressed over his heart. It was a suitably theatrical expression, one of many for which he was well-known, but the shock was genuine. Old habits die hard in an old thespian, after all.

Iain chuckled softly. He was able to see the humour in it now, if only slightly. It hadn't been quite long enough since it happened for him to have woven it into a good story, so he left it to Cliona's telling. Which was a good bit less embellished than he might have done himself.

"Aye, well. It was a near miss, that's for sure."

"Can we perhaps not talk about it?" said Cliona, her eyes downcast. Her hands were wrapped around her teacup and a small, elaborately flowered tea plate held the crumby remnants of one of Feargus' cinnamon buns. "I'd rather not have to remember how I almost killed my best friend, thank you."

"No, no, of course not," said Feargus, hurriedly. He leaned over the little table, holding up the teapot in a questioning gesture. Cliona nodded and held out her cup for a refill.

"The point is," said Feargus, "is that you simply have to pace yourself a bit. Just because it's all been left to the last minute, as it were, doesn't mean you have to try and cram years of study into a few sessions. Give yourself some time, pet. Don't let other folk, especially one of *that lot,* try and force you into things you aren't ready for."

Cliona glanced up sharply at Feargus, but he had got up from the table to replenish the plate of cinnamon buns.

"Honestly," he muttered, half under his breath. "They should

116

know better than that. I wonder if…"

Feargus paused and looked up. Cliona and Iain were watching him with quizzical looks on their faces. Bollocks, he thought. I'm doing it again.

He flapped a hand in dismissal, beaming at them with one of his hundred-watt smiles, revealing a perfect row of white teeth.

"Sorry, sorry!" he said, in a sing-song voice. "Never mind me talking to myself. Terrible habit. Sign of my advanced age, I think. Now, let's move on to brighter subjects, shall we? Did I tell you I heard from a fellow in Inverness who came across an entire set of…"

\* \* \*

Several cups of tea, a helping or two of cinnamon buns and an array of anecdotes from Feargus later, the two friends stepped out into the wind and rain. The shock of the cold, damp air after the cozy warmth of the little kitchen took their breath away. Neither said anything as they each hunched down into their coats and set off towards Mrs.Glenbogie's cottage. It was by unspoken agreement that she would have to be apprised of the events of earlier.

They found her bustling around in her own, far more antiquated, but no less welcoming kitchen. The ancient Aga pumped out a delicious warmth and the smell of something baking.

"Come in," she called, after Iain rapped on the window of the kitchen door, "It's open, pet." Her face creased into a smile when the pair walked in; a smile which faltered only slightly when she saw the expression on Cliona's face.

"Oh," she said, gripping the back of a chair with one hand and smoothing the other down her stripy apron as she attempted to dust off the flour which clung to her fingers. "Best get the kettle on, shall I?"

Iain groaned slightly.

"No thanks. We've just been to Feargus and I think I might float away. I have to be off anyway, I just wanted to see Cliona to your door. I'm sure the pair of you have lots to talk over." He glanced at Cliona who nodded, a grateful smile on her lips. She reached out and squeezed his hand. He gave a quick nod and squeezed back then turned to go.

"Hang on, love," said Mrs. Glenbogie, rummaging in one of the tins on the scrubbed worktop. She produced a half-slab of cake and proceeded to wrap it in a square of oilcloth. "Take this home for your mam. It'll do for your tea. I've got the urge to be baking and there's no way I can eat all of it."

Iain grinned, reaching out to take the parcel.

"Just a bit of my tea loaf," said Mrs. Glenbogie, smiling at the look in Iain's eyes. "I know you've a fondness for it."

"Brilliant!" said Iain, leaning over to plant a kiss on the papery cheek. "It's just the ticket." He turned to Cliona, "Let me know when you need me for the next one, aye?"

Cliona nodded, tight-lipped, without meeting his eyes. As the door closed behind him, she let out a heavy, wobbling sigh and sank into the nearest chair, as the sobs she'd been holding in finally broke loose.

"Oh, lass," said Mrs. Glenbogie, coming to stand beside her, stroking Cliona's hair as she cried. "Now what could have been as bad as all that?"

# Chapter 15

"You're right to be upset, love. It was a terrible thing, that's to be sure. Still, you can't let it stop you. You're going to have to keep going, the weather is already starting to shift."

Mrs.Glenbogie regarded Cliona's pale, tear-streaked face. Her hair hung in wild, frizzed curls around her face, having long escaped from the brightly-coloured scarf she'd used to hold it back. Dark blue smudges stood starkly from the colourlessness of her skin and her spatter of freckles stood out in sharp relief. The look of strain was evident, along with something else. It was a sort of haunted understanding. It was a look she'd seen more times than she cared to remember on Morag's face.

"But I'm guessing you already know that."

Cliona glanced up, surprise flitting across her features.

"Once you've sung the wind, it stays with you, lass. You'll have a sense of things from now on."

"I'd hardly call what I did singing the wind," said Cliona, bitterness in her voice. "It was an absolute catastrophe. And bloody dangerous. I can't put Iain at risk like that."

"I think that's the laddie's decision, don't you?"

Cliona sighed, exasperated. She ran a hand through the snarl of her hair.

"Iain has no idea how bad that could have been. He's pretending he's not scared but how could he not be? He almost went over the cliff, Mrs.G."

"Aye, you mentioned," said Eileen, getting up from the table to tend to the glorious smell emanating from the oven. "But that's over now and there's still a job to be done. And I told you that Himself would be looking after you, as he will our Iain."

Cliona snorted.

"Do you really trust him that much? I mean, it's not like he's helping us *voluntarily*, is he? If you and gran hadn't bound him all those years ago…"

Mrs. Glenbogie spoke without turning around.

"We've no choice but to trust him, nor he us. It may seem like a one-sided arrangement but there's more going on here than what we know about, lass. And before you get on your high horse about *that*, you need to accept that it's just the way of their kind to be devious and secretive. It's the only way they can survive these days."

"Oh, so we just play along while they go about their scheming and plotting? You know, I'd love to know who, or what, started this bloody mess in the first place. And no, I don't believe for a second it was just to save the honour of the sea brides, poor sods."

Cliona let herself consider that for a minute, before pulling herself back with a mental shudder. Could be worse, she allowed. I could be marrying the sea.

"Be that as it may," said Mrs. G, "our task lies in the present and that means you need to get yourself back out there and keep at it."

"But what about Iain?" said Cliona, folding her arms and

scowling. "You can't expect me to keep putting him in danger like that."

"Maybe if you worked a bit harder at doing what Skelly is trying to teach you, Iain wouldn't *be* in danger."

\* \* \*

Morag's eyes widened and she smothered a delighted smile. She sat, propped up with pillows, in her armchair by the little fire, a striped, crocheted rug over her knees, a steaming cup of tea on the little table beside her.

"Never!" she breathed, her eyes shining. "I always knew it was strong in her but, oh Eileen. She almost sent the poor lad off the cliff?"

Eileen nodded ruefully, cradling the teacup in her gnarled hands. She was wavering between terror and delight herself.

"Aye," she said. "If it weren't so horrifying, I'd have been dancing a bloody jig around the kitchen."

Morag shook her head, chuckling softly and leaned back in her chair, her eyes on the flames dancing in the grate.

"Imagine that," she said, her voice barely a whisper. "Our wee lass."

The pair of them sat in silence, each lost in her own thoughts.

"Is there time?" asked Eileen, after a moment. "Is there time for her to get control of it before the storm comes?"

Morag closed her eyes and took a deep breath. Opening them, she glanced towards the window. The black of the night did nothing to obscure the fact that the rain was still lashing down and the wind made itself known with battering certainty against the strong, stone walls of the cottage.

Sighing, she opened her eyes and looked at her old friend.

"I'm afraid that's going to depend on our girl, Eileen. If she sets her heart to it, she'll manage it just fine."

"And if she doesn't?"

Morag looked to the window again, then back to the fire.

"It's not long now," she said, her voice soft. She leaned her head back against the chair and closed her eyes. "And it's going to be a strong one."

# Chapter 16

A t Cliona's firm insistence, subsequent training sessions took place in the middle of the moor.

"I'll not have the worry if all there's to be blown about is bracken and heather," she'd said, arms folded as she glared at Skelly who glared back with equal ferocity.

"And maybe the odd sheep," interjected Iain, in an attempt to defuse the building tension.

Skelly shot him a glance which made him take several steps back. He may have looked like an old farmer but his eyes...well, his eyes didn't always match his face. Iain cleared his throat and looked down at his boots, mentally willing Cliona to *not* lose her temper.

"But you won't have the full force of the wind out here," argued Skelly. "It won't be a real test of what control you have. You need the force of the sea," he paused, taking a deep, steadying breath, "And *I* need the sea to draw on if I'm to help you."

"All the more reason to do it out here, then," said Cliona, a gleam of triumph in her eyes. "So, you don't *have* to help me. Besides, being too close to the sea isn't good for you, is it? And isn't it better if I learn to manage without you?"

Skelly's eyes narrowed.

"I think she means that it's better for her to test that she can manage on her own, that way you can be sure she's strong enough," said Iain, desperate to calm the swirling animosity.

Cliona glared at him but said nothing, before turning her attention back to Skelly. She pasted a sweet smile on her face and tilted her head.

"Iain's quite right," she said, her voice smooth. "It will be a much better measure of how well you've taught me if I can manage without too much assistance, don't you think?"

Iain turned a snort into a cough, turning his face away.

The old man pulled back his shoulders, an expression of something like resignation on his worn features; he inclined his head, regally.

"I suppose there might be some wisdom in that, lass. And you're right, it's a fair strain on me to be as close to the shore," He held up a crooked finger. "But we've got to get you back to the cliff edge once you've got your confidence out here."

Cliona nodded meekly and folded her hands in front of her.

"How would you like me to start, then?"

\* \* \*

"Do you need to lean on me?" asked Cliona, anxiously looking at her friend.

Iain limped along beside her, doing his best to take the weight off the knee which he'd twisted upon his last landing. He'd been flung, not off a cliff, but several times onto the heather which, he reasoned, was a far softer landing than the rocks.

"No," he snapped, and then immediately felt sorry. It wasn't Cliona's fault that he obviously wasn't holding up to the task.

124

"Sorry, Clee. I'm just a bit frustrated, that's all."

*"You're* frustrated?" retorted Cliona, spinning to face him. She grabbed his arm and pulled him to a halt, causing him to wince at the twist of his bad knee. "How do you think *I* feel? Hurling you about like that and no closer to managing to get a grip of things. It's a bloody good thing I kept us inland, isn't it? You'd have been sailing over the edge for sure."

Iain bit back his own, sharp-tongued response. This was classic Cliona. She was worried and frightened and so she lashed out. Still, it didn't give her the right to shout at him. All he wanted was a hot bath and a handful of aspirin and to forget he'd ever heard of wind singers or ancient faery lords masquerading as aggravating little old men. He took a deep breath.

"I'm frustrated," he began, striving to keep his voice steady and calm, "because I feel like I'm letting you down, Clee."

Cliona blinked.

"What? What do you mean?"

She gaped at Iain's face, searching it for some sign of a joke. Scowling, she turned away and started to walk back towards the cliff path. Iain limped along beside her.

"Don't be bloody ridiculous, Iain. How could you possibly be letting me down? You're up here getting battered about, aren't you?"

"Did it ever occur to you that maybe I'm not a good enough anchor? That maybe I'm getting tossed about because I'm not, I don't know, doing it right?"

"Also, ridiculous. There's no person on Glencarragh more suited to the task than you. Skelly was right about one thing, you're made of this stuff, Iain," Cliona swept an arm to encompass the expanse of moor. "You've got sea-water running through your veins for crying out loud. And you're as grounded a person as ever there was. Plus, you're my best friend in the whole world…"

Cliona's voice cracked slightly but she cleared her throat.

"No, Iain, no. This is absolutely not your fault. I'm the one with the problem. You're just the unwitting victim of my incompetence."

She gave him a wide grin, lightly punching his arm, trying to make light of the situation; trying to squash down the rising feeling of panic and dread that fought to burst out of her in screaming, hysterical tears. She was exhausted. The efforts of the afternoon had drained her completely and she felt no closer to being in proper command of the power that surged through her. And worse again, it felt like *it* was getting stronger, more in control or *her* rather than the other way around. Skelly had seen it and drilled her relentlessly, his piercing emerald eyes pitiless in the face of her frustration and fatigue. But what worried her the most, was how it felt when the wind took her; for the barest of instances, it felt good and right and she wanted nothing more than to let herself go.

Iain struggled on in silence beside her, full of his own thoughts and worries, but unwilling to voice them further. Instead, he shoved them to the back of his mind and focused on how it would feel to slide into a steaming hot bath, washing his aspirin down with a bottle of Robbie MacGregor's heather beer.

\* \* \*

"You've got post," called her mother from the kitchen. "Looks to be from one of your grand friends from school." She poked her head round the door to the utility room where Cliona was peeling off her damp mackintosh.

"Good lord, child," said Helen, taking one look at Cliona's pale face and dishevelment. "You look like you've been through the wars. Things not go well?"

Cliona merely grunted and accepted the envelope that her mother held out. A quick glance at the postmark showed it to have been sent from Paris. She swallowed hard. The internship. In all of the events of the past weeks, she'd almost forgotten about it. She surreptitiously patted the envelope, trying to discern from its thickness whether or not it was an acceptance or a rejection.

"Where is everyone?" she asked.

"They're both down at the boat," replied Helen. "Ewan's going out tomorrow and your da's helping him get the extra nets loaded."

Cliona resisted the urge to protest. Surely the weather was too unsettled to venture out just now. She kept silent. It was a futile argument and would only upset her mother.

"Cup of tea, pet?"

"That'd be lovely," replied Cliona. "I'll just go and change out of these damp things."

"Right," said Helen. "Come and have a bit to eat. I've just taken a cheese pie out of the oven. Your da and Ewan'll be ravenous when they get home."

Cliona climbed the narrow staircase to her bedroom, clutching the envelope, her thoughts running ahead of her. What if she'd been accepted? It would never come around again, it was a once in a lifetime opportunity. She pushed away all of the possible consequences of either outcome.

Every muscle ached as she pulled the damp wool of her jumper over her head. The pullover had kept her beautifully warm and dry, she mused, running her fingers over the cabled pattern before she caught herself and scowled. She was not resigned to a life of knitting jumpers, she reminded herself, even if she *had* designed some beautiful *and* functional patterns.

Sitting on the edge of her bed, she held the envelope in her cold hands, tracing the outline of the French stamp and running her finger along the seal. She sighed and looked around her attic room, taking in the simple wooden furniture - her desk and the long worktable where she'd set up her sewing machine; the dressmaker's dummy, that she'd named Eloise, which was currently sporting the half-pieced together linen pinafore smock that she was working on. She'd added large front pockets to her previous design, thinking it would be handy for foraging. Over the worktable she'd pinned sketches and fabric swatches, photographs and images torn from magazines, including a glossy postcard depicting the Eiffel Tower.

Shivering, she reached over and pulled a periwinkle blue shawl from where it lay across her pillow. Mrs.Glenbogie had made it for her eighteenth birthday and it was fantastically warm, despite being very light. She wrapped it around herself, tucking her nose into its soft warmth. The wind rattled the windows, making it sound like a someone was trying to get in. She got up and tugged on the sash, making sure it was properly closed. Rain streaked down the warped glass, blurring the view over the rooftops and down to the sea. Cliona pressed her forehead against the icy pane and closed her eyes against the dull ache that was rising from the back of her neck.

Best just get on with it, then, she told herself with a heavy sigh. She grabbed a knitting needle from the workbasket and slid it under the seal.

# Chapter 17

In the dream, she was down at the shore, collecting sea glass. A voice called her name and she turned to see a blonde woman who, in her dream, she recognized as a dear friend. Smiling, she stood up and waved, feeling as she did so an enormous sense of relief washing over her. Things were going to be okay after all.

She woke up with a start, blinking in the grey light of the morning, as she tried to sort out where she was. Only minutes ago, she'd been down at the beach, hadn't she? And who was that other woman? She wracked her brain trying to place her. Was it someone from university, making a guest appearance? She looked so familiar. Cliona closed her eyes again, half-wanting to go back into the dream to find out. Also, her room was freezing, and she was reluctant to come out from her burrow of duvet and blankets.

The sound of voices wound their way into her doze, and she groaned gently, knowing she was going to have to get up and face the day. Besides, she wanted to try and talk Ewan into not taking the boat out. Not that it would make any difference whatsoever, but she had to at least try. With a deep breath of determination, she flung off the insulating layers and forced herself to sit up. As she did so, nausea washed over her in a sickening wave and a sharp pain flashed behind her eyes. Gasping, she brought the heels of her hands to her eyes, doubling over as she forced herself to breathe. It passed as quickly as it had come, and slowly, tentatively, she sat up.

*Now what?* she muttered to herself as she pulled on layers of clothing. Woolen tights and a long-sleeved linen dress over a long-sleeved thermal knit and her vintage-styled petticoat, followed by the pullover she'd worn the day before. She contemplated bringing Mrs.G's shawl but thought it might be overkill. It was bound to be warmer downstairs. She had her hand on her doorknob when she changed her mind and grabbed the shawl off the bed, wrapping it tightly around her body and tying it behind her back.

\* \* \*

"You're up early," commented Ewan, smirking as he glanced at the clock.

Cliona stuck out her tongue, refusing to look and see what time it was. She didn't keep a clock in her bedroom for the exact reason she wasn't looking at one now. She'd told herself that if she was forced to be in Glencarragh then she would live the life of the artless bohemian.

"I didn't know Feargus was putting on a production," continued Ewan, idly buttering a slice of toast.

He'd probably been out at the boat before dawn and had come home for breakfast, thought Cliona, refusing to feel guilty.

"Do you think it'll help your chances?" He looked pointedly at her outfit, a glint of mischief twinkling in his eyes. "You know, looking the part already and that."

Cliona gave him a withering stare but said nothing. Normally she'd be happy to do a nice round of verbal jousting, but she was feeling decidedly uneasy and it was distracting. She glanced up at the kitchen window but beyond the streaming rain, there was nothing to see.

"Never you mind, Ewan," said Helen, placing a large steaming mug of tea in front of Cliona. "There's more to the world than Arran jumpers and corduroys, you know. Maybe if you'd ever venture off this blessed rock, you'd see more of what the young people are doing these days with their fashion. It might surprise you to know that folk do all kinds of strange things. Isn't that right, pet?"

Cliona gave her mother a grateful, amused smile, burying her face in the steam from her mug. Her stomach lurched defiantly, and she gritted her teeth against the pain in her head.

"Are you alright, lass?" asked Ewan, giving her a worried frown. "Only you look a bit peaky."

Cliona forced a smile and nodded, forcing air through her nose. She took a sip of tea which instantly settled the hollowness in her belly. Maybe she was just hungry. She couldn't remember if she'd eaten anything substantial yesterday.

"Where's Da?" she asked, looking at his empty chair by the fire.

"He's down at the boat," replied Ewan, standing up and brushing toast crumbs off his well-darned jumper. "Which is where I best get to if I'm going to catch the afternoon tide. Oh, ta very much,"

He accepted the flask of tea which Helen was holding out, along with a packet of sandwiches.

"Just in case you both get a bit peckish before you head out."

Ewan leaned over and placed a kiss on his mother's cheek then turned back to Cliona, who was half out of her chair.

"You surely can't be going out today?" said Cliona, gripping the edge of the table as the nausea rose again. "It's vile out there. Did you check the storm tracker?"

Ewan gave her an indulgent smile.

"Of course, I did, and so did our da. And as he's fond of saying, you can't always rely on some foolish computer gadget to be accurate around the island. Besides, if I don't get out today, I'll miss the window then I *will* be in a pickle."

"But Iain said even the pelagic trawler won't go out right now. They're holding back for another week."

"Aye, well," said Ewan, scowling as he made his way to the door, "I daresay whatever conglomerate it is that owns that bloody trawler can afford to miss a few dances. Us small fellows have to take what we can when the opportunity arises, right?"

Without waiting for her response, he slammed out the door.

"Why do you challenge them so?" asked Helen, clearing away the breakfast dishes.

Cliona sat down, huddling over her tea. She shook her head.

"Because one day they're going to come to grief over their stubbornness. Over *Da's* stubbornness. Ewan has had numerous offers from the tour boat company, but he knows Da wouldn't have it. He could captain his own boat. He's as good as Iain, maybe better. And if he still feels the call of the haddock he can just sign onto the trawler from time to time. They're always looking for good men."

A pronounced silence made her look up. Her mother stared at her with disbelief in her eyes, her hands paused halfway to picking up a jar of jam.

"What?" said Cliona, defensive. "I'm sorry if this classes as

133

causing a stir, but it's true."

"The call of the haddock?" repeated Helen, her mouth quirking into a wide smile.

Cliona opened her mouth and closed it again, unsure of how to respond. She'd been known to go too far, and her family didn't always appreciate the way she saw things.

Helen's shoulders shook as silent laughter bubbled up. Soon, they were both clutching each other as tears rolled down their cheeks.

\* \* \*

The dull ache in her head and the churning of her stomach accompanied her for most of the morning. Finally, unable to stand it any longer, she decided to go and visit her gran, hoping she'd have a brew of some sort that would help. She switched off her sewing machine and shuffled the pieces of fabric into an untidy pile, her hand brushing against a stack of paper as she did so. She cursed softly as the pile slid to the floor, and then not so softly at the effect of leaning down to pick them up had on her head. The Paris postmark caught her eye and she paused, staring at the envelope for a moment before sighing and shoving it back into the pile. She had no inclination to deal with that at present.

"I'm just off to see Gran," she called as she passed through the kitchen.

"Give her my love," called her mother from somewhere in the sitting room. "Ask her for tea, will you? I'm worried she's not eating."

"Will do."

Cliona felt instant relief as she stepped out into the cold, damp air. Breathing in great lungfuls of the salt wind, she felt her head ease slightly. Fresh air, she mused, quoting Mrs.Glenbogie, a tonic for what ails you.

She was halfway down the hill to the village when it hit her. A piercing pain flashed behind her eyes and a tidal wave of nausea sent her staggering to the bushes at the side of the path. She emptied her stomach and stood, hands on her knees, doubled over, pale and sweating. But beyond the physical sensation, there was something else. Something that pulled and tugged. Something that burned with a firm, steady, rhythmic insistence. She squeezed her eyes closed, trying to quell the rising panic that came along with the other, unknown and yet still, somehow, recognizable feeling.

"No," she whispered. "No, not now."

She forced herself to straighten, sheer effort of will crushing down the sensations that rolled through her. She continued on down the hill, focusing on the bite of the rain as the wind hurled it at her face, her mind firm on getting to her grandmother's cottage. *Gran will know what to do*, she thought, almost in a whimper. *I can't do this.*

She was almost there when another surge ran through her, leaving her gasping and heaving. The wind swirled around her, taunting.

*Best get ready, lass. It won't be long now. Surely you can feel it?*

Skelly's voice echoed through her thoughts but Cliona was already running.

\* \* \*

135

"It's coming," said Cliona.

Iain stopped what he was doing, the piece of sandpaper held motionless in his hands. Carefully, he set it down and stepped off the stool he'd been standing on to reach the hull of the dry-docked boat. Outside, the wind gusted, rattling the loose panes of the boathouse window, sending a shrieking whistle through the cracks in the wooden slats of the walls. He cast a quick look behind her, toward the open door where he could see the first fat drops of rain staining the quayside.

"Are you sure?" he asked. "Will your Gran…"

Cliona shook her head, biting her lip to stop it trembling.

"No," she whispered. "She's not very strong just now. But Mrs. Glenbogie says that between them, they can offer something." Her voice faltered. She cleared her throat and straightened her shoulders.

"She said I'll have to do it on my own."

"What? But you've never done it before, Cliona. Surely they can't expect you to manage on your own!"

Cliona laughed, a hollow, mirthless sound. The memory of Skelly's warnings flashing through her mind.

Then she looked at Iain. His face was creased with concern, but his eyes were steady on hers. She felt the strength of him and his convictions. She held out her hand.

"Well, I'll not exactly be alone, will I?"

# Chapter 18

"You can't be serious?"

Cliona's voice rose to drown out the shrieking wind. Her hair had escaped from underneath her mackintosh hood and clung in wet strands against her pale skin. Her eyes were wide with incredulity and fear.

"Please, Ewan? Will you not listen to reason? Surely you remember the last time there was a storm this bad. You know it's not.... normal."

Cliona gripped her brother's sleeve. He shook her hand away, brushing her aside as he moved around the shed, collecting the spare net.

"What are you on about, silly lass?" he said, smiling grimly at his younger sister. "A storm is a storm is a storm according to our da and I'm fair sick of arguing with him about it."

"Tell me you're not doing this just to get one back at him? Ewan, it's madness. You know it is. It's not worth it. Please listen to me."

Cliona clung to his arm, pleading.

"You've nothing to prove, Ewan."

Her brother gently, but firmly removed her hand from his arm again.

"Don't worry so, lass. Aye, it's a waste of time and fuel trying to go out in this. But the old man insists the fish will be stirred up by the storm and that all I have to do is get out past the edge of it. I've argued 'til I'm blue in the face but he's a stubborn sod and all the fighting is wearing down our mam. I'm all for the easy life, aye? I'll go out, get soaked and come home with no fish. Maybe that'll shut the bugger up."

"But it's not a normal storm! Surely you remember the last time this happened. What about Joe Ashton?"

Cliona saw the look on her brother's face and immediately regretted what she'd said. Joe Ashton had been caught out in the last great faery storm; pieces of his boat had washed up on the north shore of the island but his body had never been recovered.

"Don't you be talking of the lost, Cliona Stewart," said Ewan, scowling. He bundled the loops of net into one hand as he crossed himself hurriedly with the other. "You know fair well it's nothing but ill to invoke the sea-taken before a fisherman sets out, regardless of the circumstances."

"But you can't go out. That's my point," wailed Cliona. "It's going to be a bad one. And gran can't sing so I'm stuck not knowing what I'm doing with just Iain and Sk…"

"Never mind that, my girl," said a stern voice behind them.

Whirling around, Cliona turned to face her father. Donal Stewart stood with his arms folded in the doorway of the shed. His broad shoulders spanned the entire door frame and his face was clouded with anger.

"I've told you time and again, lass," he said, his voice low, but tinged with a controlled fury. "I'll not have any of that superstitious nonsense in my house or around this boat."

"But Da!"

Forgetting all reservations surrounding her father's rage,

Cliona stepped toward him and clasped her hands, pleading silently. "It's not a normal storm. It's a faery storm. Gran…"

Holding up his hand, he stopped her with a look.

"No, Cliona. I'll not have it. Your Gran's not well and it's making her talk more foolishly than ever. Now, leave us to what needs doing. Your brother has work to do if he's going to catch the turning tides, aye?"

"It's alright, Cliona," said Ewan. Setting down the nets, he took Cliona in a quick hug, tucking a wild strand of sodden hair back behind her ear. He looked into her eyes, willing her to see reason. "I'm fine. Truly."

Stepping back, he pulled a knitted hat from his back pocket. "Besides," he said with a grin, casting a quick glance at the thunderous face of their father. "What better occasion to try out my new hat if not the promise of a grand big catch, aye? When we're sitting comfy round the fire this winter, our bellies as full as our cupboards, we can say it was Cliona's knitting that favoured the last big haul of the season, right?"

\* \* \*

Morag lay on the narrow bed, propped up on pillows. Her soup mug was empty, and everything had been said, but the effort of it had drained the last of her energy. The skin of her face was pallid, and her breathing came in rasps, but her eyes danced as they'd looked at her granddaughter.

"Och, you've grown into such a bonny lass. Hasn't she, Eileen?"

Eileen smiled at Cliona from her seat beside her old friend's bed. She squeezed Morag's frail wrist gently. "Aye, Morag, she has that!"

Cliona tried to smile in response, but her face felt numb and she had developed a strangely disjointed feeling, as if her head wasn't attached to her body.

"That's the normal way of it," Gran had told her, when Cliona had arrived, pale and shaken and terrified. "The sick feeling and the headache, it's the storm, you see? You've got a bit of the wild magic in you now and it doesn't rest easy in a mortal soul."

She'd smiled and smoothed a gentle hand over Cliona's wind-ravaged hair.

"As you know, the wind won't come willing. It's a wild thing, aye? That's one of the reasons why we need the glass, it helps to boost what little we have."

She tapped the bundle of linen containing the selkie glass that Mrs.Glenbogie had given Cliona earlier.

"It's good that you've not had to use it yet. It means it's still got the full strength in it."

She paused, closing her eyes briefly and taking a breath. After a moment, she opened them again and looked into her granddaughters frightened face. She smiled, feeling her heart breaking with the memory of how she'd felt, all those years ago.

"It'll get easier, *mo chroi,* but not for a while. Just keep your heart on the earth. It'll hold you, and your Iain. He's a good lad; he's strong with the land and with you. You couldn't have made a better choice. And let Himself in, full and proper like. It'll terrify you, but it's the only way he can help, and we just can't manage without him anymore."

Morag gave Eileen a worried glance and sighed.

"She's just too strong."

"It'll be alright, pet. Don't you worry," whispered Morag as Cliona kneeled against her bed, her head buried in the eiderdown quilt as she wept. Morag smoothed her gnarled fingers through Cliona's bright curls. "Everything will be alright in the end."

# Chapter 19

"We can't go up there, Cliona," shouted Iain above the roar of the wind. "We'll be blown off the edge, forchrissakes!"

Cliona clutched the top rail of the stile that barred the path leading up to the cliff edge. The rain was blowing across the moor in cold blasts, soaking them both, despite the oilskins that Iain had insisted they take from the cupboard in the tour boat shed. Her face was pinched with strain and her eyes stood stark against the paleness of her skin. She trembled visibly and waves of nausea rolled through her with every crack of thunder from across the sea. The weight of the glass in her mackintosh pocket lay heavy against her hip. She tried to quell her roiling stomach and pounding headache with visions of her gran and Mrs. Glenbogie, as she'd last seen them, hands locked together, beginning the low hum of the wind-song in the warm, fire-lit kitchen of her Gran's cottage. She thought of Ewan, loading the nets onto the rolling deck of their boat.

"If you really want to help me, Iain," said Cliona through blue-tinged lips. "You'll go down to the quay and stop my brother from getting in that boat."

"He what? Why would he do that? It's madness! Hasn't he read the storm report? Surely your da won't let him go."

Iain stared in disbelief at the distant harbor. Through the murky curtain of rain, the tethered boats were just visible. They bobbed wildly up and down on the moorings, bright splashes of blue and white and red against the mottled grey-black of the angry sea and the strange green glow of the storm-wild sky.

Cliona shook her head.

"My da doesn't believe in the storms, Iain," bitterly. "He's convinced that it's a narrow band and Ewan'll pass right through it to the biggest catch of the year."

She let go of the stile long enough to grip Iain's arm. "He's going to go out, Iain. Just to prove my da wrong. Please…if you want to help me, don't let my brother go out in this."

Letting go of his arm, she groaned and pressed the heel of her hand to her forehead.

"I'll be alright," she glanced towards the top of the cliff. Something was pulling her there, insisting that that was where she needed to be.

Iain stared wildly between Cliona and the harbour. Finally, he shook his head.

"No," he said, his voice firm and steady. "I'm staying with you."

But Cliona wasn't listening, her eyes were vague and unfocused.

"I have to go now. I'll be alright," she repeated. "Skelly's here."

\* \* \*

The wind lashed the trees into a frenzy, sending their branches flailing as they made their way up the cliff path. Cliona was only faintly aware of Iain's presence; she could feel herself deepening into the hum that seemed to rise from the earth beneath her feet.

The rain blew in sideways sheets, stabbing like a million cold needles against the bare skin of her face. Her hair had torn free of her hood again and whipped like a live thing around her, blinding her with its sodden strands.

"I can't do it," she whispered through numb lips. Tears mingled with rain on her face and she shuddered with cold and despair. "I can't…"

The voice in her head was calm but firm.

*Aye, lass. You can. You have to.*

They trudged onwards, hunched into the collar of their oilskins, hands clenched into tight fists. Cliona found herself humming, an old sea-farer's ballad that Ewan always sang after the harvest festival meal in the village hall.

A movement flickered at the corner of her eye and she paused in her steady march. Iain walked onward, oblivious. The lashing rain blurred her vision but there, huddled against a large boulder was the figure of a small child.

Cliona blinked, wiping a hand across her face to stem the streaming rain.

Surely there wouldn't be a child out in weather like this. She must be seeing things. She allowed herself to look back, down the hill toward the village streets. Squares of warm, yellow light spilled from windows. The folk of Glencarragh had lit their storm lamps.

Turning back, she saw the small figure move slightly. There was definitely something there. She moved closer, calling out as she did so.

"Hello? Are you alright?"

A low whimpering sound came from the huddled form. As

Cliona reached it, she saw that it wasn't actually a child, but a very small man, clothed in tattered rags. In the dying light, she saw his skin was a mottled brownish-green; his eyes, large and liquid black, gazed fearfully at her from strangely angled features.

"Selkie," she breathed, not daring to believe it. She reached out a trembling hand, enchanted and drawn to the shivering form. She felt a strange surge of affection.

The creature recoiled from her gesture, the whimper becoming a low moan.

Cliona reached into the oilskin to her mackintosh pocket. Her fingers brushed over the smooth, sea-polished surfaces of the glass that she found there. Selkie glass, to infuse the wind-song. Heaven knew she was going to need all the help she could get. Swallowing hard, she withdrew the largest piece and held it out to the little man.

His liquid eyes widened, and he hesitated only slightly before reaching out to grab the glass. There was an eerie wail accompanied the sound of scrabbling feet as the creature darted towards the cliff edge.

"Nooo!" shouted Cliona, fearful that the selkie was bolting blindly. But she needn't have worried. Several feet from the edge of the cliff, the air blurred and shimmered and the long, sinuous shape of a seal arched in the air before disappearing over the edge.

Cliona stood staring blankly as the storm raged around her.

*Thank you, lass,* said the voice in her head. *That was a kindness that won't be forgotten.*

Cliona shuddered and resumed her trek up the path. She caught up with Iain who simply turned to her and gave her a smile of grim reassurance, as if not noticing she hadn't been beside him all along. The lure of the cliff edge was stronger than she wanted to acknowledge; for a brief moment, she envied the selkie-man and his leap to freedom. He knew where he belonged.

Finally, they reached the top. As the wind shrieked across moor, Cliona, exhausted, dropped to her knees and dug her fingers into the mossy grass, clinging to the earth as the sea raged against the rocks below. Iain placed himself beside her, spreading his booted feet and tamping them down into the grass. He leaned down and gave her shoulder a firm squeeze. Nodding, she leaned her head against his arm for a brief moment. Neither of them spoke.

*Skelly?* she moaned, as waves of nausea rolled over her. She found herself wishing that Iain wasn't there, that she had sent him away. How could she have risked his safety? Too many of the people she loved were already in danger.

*Help me.*

*I'm here, lass. I'll do everything I can for you, but you've got to let me in.*

# Chapter 20

Wave after wave of nausea hit her. She no longer felt the sting of the wind and rain, just the searing pain behind her eyes and the lurching of her stomach. Dizzy, she dug her fingers more tightly into the soil on the cliff's edge.

"Okay," she whispered, her voice drowned by the wind and rain. "Do what you have to do. But please, help me."

She felt him, rather than heard his voice; his presence was stronger now, than when he'd come to her before. She tasted salt on her tongue and smelled the tang of seaweed and fish and the dark of the ocean. Then, a slow warmth crept through her cold flesh, bringing feeling back to her rain-drenched skin and chasing away the despair.

Somewhere, from very far away, she felt her gran and Mrs. Glenbogie. A low hum started from a place deep inside her and there were flashes of color at the edges of her vision.

*Get up, lass,* he said. *It's alright now. You can't come to harm. I've got you now. Me and your laddie will hold you. But you've got to sing for me. For my people and yours. Don't let us go, aye?"*

"Where are you?" she asked, aloud, the nausea gone and her head clear. She stood tall, just back from the cliff's edge, untouched by the wind and rain, gazing down at the heaving sea and night-black sky. Around her, the trees and shrubs bent low against the thrashing wind, clinging to the earth by the roots that had held them through countless other storms. Iain stood beside her, his eyes closed in concentration, fists clenched and his beautiful Glencarragh features pale with strain.

*I'm where you need me to be, lass,* said Skelly. *But we've work to do, aye? Let's put an end to it.*

\* \* \*

She still had no idea how or what she was doing. The words came to her from somewhere far inside herself, from a place she never knew was there.

"You'll just know," her Gran had said. "It's a deep knowing that you have. You've got the gift of it, lass. That's as much as we understand. None of us know the how or the where. Just that it's older than time and it's there, waiting. When you need it, it'll happen."

Skelly had told her much the same - nothing helpful or practical, just that she'd know what to do when she needed to do it.

She felt outside herself. It was as if she was a *part* of the wind; she felt the strength of it and the glory of its untethering. More than anything she wanted to give herself over to the wildness, to break apart into a million pieces and scatter herself, her very being, into all of the places the wind could take her. It would be the ultimate leave-taking.

A great surge of power ran through her and suddenly she saw herself, head flung back and arms wide, as she stood singing, not beside Iain, but standing on the edge of the cliff. Her hair blew in a fury around her head and a nimbus of blue-white light glowed around her.

*Easy, lass,* said Skelly, a note of warning in his voice. *Don't let go. Get back with your anchor. You're letting it carry you too much. Don't listen to her.*

His voice was just a distant echo. She'd lost the sound of her gran and Eileen, but she wasn't afraid anymore. Their presence had been a comfort, but she didn't need them now. Now, she had full control of the wind.

"Yes, my love," said a strange voice from behind her. "You can feel it, can't you?"

Cliona spun around to face a tall, willowy form that flickered as the wind spun and whirled. A strangely beautiful, dark-haired woman dressed in a long, shimmering cloak the colour of the Glencarragh sea stood in the lee of the contorted hawthorn, her long-fingered hand resting on the arched, muscular neck of a massive black horse. The horse's red eyes were wide, nostrils flared. A thick tangle of ropy black mane cascaded almost to the ground and was unmoved by the wind.

"Who..." began Cliona, her own eyes wide. The thrumming grew steadily stronger and she felt herself gaining momentum. Electric tingles shot down her arms to the tips of her fingers, she felt her attention stray back to the cliff edge.

The woman regarded Cliona with a calculating stare. She looked around her, a curious smirk crossing her beautiful features when she saw Iain standing, hunched now against the force of the wind.

"You are not alone, after all." she said, more of a statement than a question. "Interesting."

"Who are you?" Cliona asked again.

149

"A friend," said the woman, shaking back her mass of gleaming black hair, "that is all." The horse shifted his weight, stretching its long, sinuous neck towards Cliona as it blew softly through blood-red nostrils. "A friend who would see you free of the binding that has been thrust upon you."

The woman tilted her head, her sharp, angular features curious. Her eyes were a grey-green, but the colour shifted and swirled, like clouds scudding across a storm-leaden sky.

"Free?" croaked Cliona, the words getting stuck in her throat.

"Yes," crooned the woman, her tone softening into a sing-song lilt. "Wouldn't you like to be carried away from here, from this prison of stone and moor?"

She gestured, a long arm escaping from the folds of her sea-coloured cloak. Cliona saw that her blue-grey skin was covered in shimmering scales.

Cliona followed the gesture, her vision clearing into a view across the moor, inland to the fens and bogs; to the shepherd's crofts and clumps of craggy forest that should never had been able to survive the punishing winds. She looked away, down the cliff path towards the village, where her own house stood, and those of her gran and Iain and Mrs. Glenbogie. In her mind's eye, she saw the brightly-coloured fishing boats, bobbing on their moorings and heard the shouts of fishermen, calling out in greeting or good-natured jest. The tea shop, The Oracle, Dorothy McShane's gift shop where she'd just the other day dropped off a basket of knitted socks and hats for her mother. It all passed behind her eyes like a cinema reel.

It would be so easy. The wind was wild in her and here was someone who understood what it was to feel tethered to a place, without a choice to make a life of her own.

She turned back to the woman, who stood, a small smile

playing over her lips.

"No! Cliona!"

Her gran's voice was a shout from somewhere inside her head. But it was hard to feel where she was, and Cliona wasn't sure she even wanted to. The storm raged through her now; it had become a part of her. She had, after all, called it to herself. She was a part of it, and it was magnificent! She stopped caring that she couldn't hear her gran and that Skelly seemed to have gone. She wondered, briefly, who they were.

Suddenly, a jolt of electricity shot through her and she felt a sharp pain in her head. She staggered, knocked off balance by a gust of wind, and fell to her knees.

Lights flashed behind her eyes - images flickering like lightning. People she'd known, only from photographs behind glass - the fishermen's memorial. She felt the choke of seawater, the burn of salt and the panic of being held under. Thunder cracked like a gunshot above her head and the rain came in sheets, numbing her face and hands.

Through it all, the wind song thrummed. She could feel the vibration of it; rising from deep within her, coming up from the earth and through her body.

She saw the looming waves poised above the decks of fishing boats, heard the scream of timber and the cries of men thrown into the sea. All around them, as the fishermen struggled to rise to the churning surface, she saw the strange faces of creatures who dwelt in the sea. Sharp-toothed grins and long, tendril fingers that reached out to pluck at the clothing of the drowning men.

From somewhere, close by but far away at the same time, Cliona heard the enraged shriek of a woman. The woman with the horse, she mused, detaching herself for a moment from the terror of the screams. She let herself be led into the silence of the magic. It would have been so easy to stay there, sheltering from the battle that was raging around her.

But the faces of the drowned men returned; they became those of her friends and family.

She shuddered and pressed her forehead into the rain-soaked moss, willing the visions to disappear as she pulled the song from somewhere deep in the earth. She could hear her gran again, her voice strong and solid in her mind. Not only that but the song of generations of women reached out and joined her own, bolstering it as she struggled against the horrors of what she saw and felt.

The strength of the wind had shifted; she held it again, but apart from her this time, not from within. She trembled with the effort; it was so much harder this way. It would be easier to move into it; to let it the silence take her. She felt herself slipping, the taste of wildness thrilling through her again. She saw the smiling face of the beautiful woman with her red-eyed horse.

*Cliona.*

Skelly's voice was quietly, barely there. *More, lassie,* he said, faintly. *She's too strong...*

The wind surged again, ripping itself from her grasp. She felt Skelly, struggling. She felt, rather than heard, her gran cry out.

A swell of seawater surged into her face. Coughing, she spluttered and gasped, the salt burning her nose and throat. She could hear the clanging of bells and see the sweep of the lighthouse beam. The boat rose and fell, like a horse bucking. Her feet slipped and she crashed to the deck.

"Noooo," she moaned, back on the cliff edge. The images

flashed behind her tightly closed eyes. She saw the familiar nets, recognizing the way her grandad had taught her to knot the charms into the heavy rope. The lanterns she'd painted swung wildly in the buffeting wind and she smelled the kerosene from the small stove Ewan had taken to make tea and heat the cheese pie that their mam had baked the day before.

"Please..." she whispered, reaching out for Skelly, for her gran and Eileen, and the other women, but they were gone. She swung a hand, sweeping the air around her, trying to find Iain, but he was meters away, down on his hands and knees shouting her name. In one final effort she dug her hand into the pocket of her coat. The glass burned as she touched it, searing the skin on the palm of her hand. The wind shrieked and she heard the crack and splinter of wood.

The sea closed over her head and she screamed.

# Chapter 21

Jimmy Ferguson found them where they had fallen.

Cliona's skin was bleached white and she was shuddering with cold, her hair plastered to her face. She was curled up in a ball, her hands clenched into fists, bunching the periwinkle blue shawl that Mrs.Glenbogie had knit for her eighteenth birthday. She was quietly murmuring the words of an old, fisherman's prayer.

Iain lay a few feet away in a crumpled heap at the base of the hawthorn tree.

The wind had dropped to gentle gusts and the rain pattered softly on the soggy ground, streaking the black trunk of the stunted hawthorn until it shone in the light of the morning.

"Cliona?" said Jimmy, breathless from his rushed climb to the top of the steep incline. He'd not long been back in his grandfather's croft before Eileen Glenbogie had banged on the door at first light, begging him to get another group together. He knelt down beside her, putting a strong hand on her sodden shoulder.

"Are you alright, lass?" his voice wavering slightly with fatigue and grief. He looked up, frowning and directed the other men of the search party towards the still form of Iain.

No, he thought. Please, God, not another one.

Cliona spoke without opening her eyes.

"Ewan's dead," she said. "He's dead and it's all my fault."

\* \* \*

"It's alright, pet," said Eileen, stroking a gentle hand down Cliona's cold, wet, face as she handed her a mug of steaming tea. Her own face was worn and tired, and she had to stop and lean on the wooden dresser on her way back to her own chair.

"How can it be alright?" asked Cliona, her voice barely above a whisper. "How can you even say that?"

"Because I know it to be true," replied Eileen, shrugging her shawl tightly around her shoulders. "The sea..."

Cliona slammed the mug down on the table, sloshing tea across her hand. She barely noticed the burning liquid.

"Don't talk to me about the sea!" she shouted. "I don't want any more of your stories and nothing of your feeble acceptance of the way things are supposed to be!"

"Cliona..." began Iain, reaching across to touch her arm. A large bruise was spreading over the side of his face from where he'd been thrown against the hawthorn and it stood out in stark relief of his own bloodless features.

She shook off his touch and stood up, letting the tartan woolen blanket fall from her shoulders into a heap on the floor.

"No, Iain. I've had enough. What happened last night...I can't...," her voice was choked with emotion. Taking a deep breath, she wrapped her arms around her waist, hugging the periwinkle shawl to herself. It had remained remarkably dry and she clung to its soft comfort. "I will not be responsible for

155

any more deaths," she said quietly. "Clearly, I'm not suitable to the task." She held up her hand as Eileen opened her mouth to speak. "You've got the wrong person, Mrs. Glenbogie. I won't be doing this again."

With that, she spun around and ran out, letting the kitchen door slam shut behind her.

Inside the tiny kitchen, the only sound was the ticking of the clock and the burbling hiss of the old Aga. Somewhere, outside, a cat meowed.

Iain sighed and pushed back his chair.

"No, lad," said Eileen. "Let her go. She needs some time to sort it all out,"

"But what if she's right? What if she's not up to it? And you can't expect her to bear the burden of Ewan and her gran all by herself!"

"Ewan made his choice," said Eileen. "As cold-hearted as it may sound, in the end it was him and him alone as chose to try and pass through the storm and neither Cliona nor yourself could have turned him from it. If there's a burden of guilt to be borne, then it rests on Donal Stewart, not our wee lass. There's some folk that no matter how many times they're beaten over the head with the reality of things, they don't want to listen. Blind and foolish! That's always been the trouble with Donal Stewart"

"That's all very academic, Mrs. Glenbogie," said Iain, frowning at the door. "But you can't think for a minute that Cliona will accept it as sufficient."

Eileen shook her head.

"No, lad. Maybe not just now, no. But she will."

She leaned over and patted his hand.

"And don't worry, pet. Morag's not quite ready to go just yet, and she'll see right by the lass before she does."

\* \* \*

Cliona sat in the dim sitting room. The window was open just a crack, letting in the cool, damp, sea air that both her gran and Eileen swore was a tonic for all that ever ailed a body. The oil lamp in the corner cast a muted yellow glow, smoothing the sharp edges of her gran's face into deep shadows and smudges while the fire crackled quietly in the soot-blackened hearth. The eiderdown rose and fell, with each faint and rasping breath as Morag dozed.

"Oh, Gran," whispered, Cliona. "What have I done?"

Morag opened her eyes.

"Ah, pet. You've done everything you were needed to do," she said in a frail whisper.

Cliona lifted her bowed head.

"You're awake!" she smiled through her tears. "I never thought I'd…"

Morag chuckled, a wheezy sound like dried grass in the wind.

"Och, lass. You'd not think I'd move on without a word, would you? Oh, now. Don't start the sobbing again, there's naught to be grieving for where I'm concerned, aye? I'm ready to go, lass. I have been for a while now. I was just hanging on to get you through the first storm."

Cliona's shoulders slumped and she avoided her Gran's eye.

"I know about Ewan, love. I knew as soon as you knew. Skelly…."

At the mention of his name, Cliona's head snapped up. Her eyes flashed with anger and she gripped the folds of her still-damp coat tightly.

"Don't talk to me about him," she said, sharply. "I thought he was supposed to help us. I thought he was supposed to protect us from the storm. Why didn't he save Ewan?" she finished, her voice breaking.

Morag smiled gently. Her face creased into a hundred folds and the corners of her eyes crinkled. She pulled her hand from under the eiderdown and took Cliona's cold one in hers.

"He did help us, pet."

"How can that be? We lost Ewan. *I* lost Ewan. A soul for a soul, you said. He protects ours in exchange for us protecting his. Have we let one of his people die? Have we not kept our end of the bargain?" Cliona sobbed, eyes wild, teetering on hysteria. She stood up and started pacing around the room, wringing her hands.

"Sit down, lass. I've got something to tell you."

Cliona sat down on the edge of the bed, next to her Gran. The old woman seemed to have faded right before her eyes. Biting back tears, she pushed a wisp of white hair back from Morag's face and tucked the edge of the eiderdown more tightly around her tiny frame.

"Skelly did save a soul tonight, *mo ghrá.*"

"What do you mean?"

"He saved yours."

\* \* \*

"How're you holding up?" asked Iain as they walked along the edge of the sea. The day was bright and clear, the sea rippling over the sand in a gentle, undulating rhythm that soothed.

Cliona tucked her hand tightly into the crook of his elbow and leaned in slightly, glad for his presence and his quiet strength. There were no illusions with Iain, no pretense of how she might be feeling. He knew, after all, what she was and what she'd done and offered his friendship regardless.

"Oh, you know!" she said, trying for joviality. "Two funerals in as many weeks, we won't have to cook for the next three months, all the food that's in our deep freeze!"

Iain smiled and squeezed her hand.

A gull skimmed across the surface of the sea, keening into the breeze. An answering cry came from higher along the cliff and a second gull joined the first as they flew out towards the open sea.

"Have you talked to your da?" he asked.

"Da isn't talking to anyone," she replied. "He just sits and stares into the fire and mutters."

"Oh, he'll come around, I suppose. With time," said Iain, not quite believing it. He had seen it happen before. The grief of losing someone to the sea had a different edge to it. Like a child being attacked by the family dog, it was a betrayal of trust and a hurt that ran deeper than the injury. The fact that Ewan's body hadn't been recovered only made the matter worse.

Cliona knew the same. She shrugged, not saying anything.

They walked in silence for a while, not really planning on going anywhere, as long as it wasn't back to the house. Neither of them could bear the kind words and condolences. The strained quiet and hush of funeral gatherings didn't seem to fit with the memory of Morag.

"She would've preferred a party," Cliona had argued with her mother. Her mother was pale and tired and simply stared at her daughter. Cliona was instantly sorry. Of course, they couldn't have a party. Not so soon after losing Ewan.

Eileen hadn't attended the funeral.

"I'll mourn in my own way," she had assured Cliona. "Besides," she'd added, with a mischievous sparkle in her eye, "I don't think my old friend will ever be far from me. Not if I know her at all!"

"Has he…" said Iain, as they turned around at the end of the strand, unable to go any further past the base of the cliff because of the rising tide.

"Skelly?" said Cliona, quickly. "No, he's not…here," she waved a hand, gesturing toward her head, laughing a little at the notion of it.

"Gran said he'd be away for a while. That the strain of…. of the night…would've taken a toll on him."

Iain nodded.

"You're not still angry with him?" he asked.

"No, I don't suppose I can be. After all, it was Gran who pushed him to make the choice, in the end. And she gave up…well, she did what she thought was best, I suppose. If I'd been able to hold the storm properly, then maybe it would have ended differently."

Cliona frowned down at her feet. They were retracing their footprints. Each step imprinting on the opposite direction, they overstepped where they had trodden before. Soon, the tide would creep in and wash those away too.

"Gran said I'm not to feel guilty about what happened. She said it wasn't my fault. About Ewan, that is. And Mrs. Glenbogie said the same." She spoke out towards the expanse of the ocean, as if trying to convince herself.

"And they'd be right." said Iain. "There's more good to come of you *not* having flown off with the wind, isn't there? And

Ewan was a grown man and an experienced fisherman. He made his choice."

Cliona gave a small, sad smile that didn't quite reach her eyes.

"That's what they all keep telling me. But what I know in my head doesn't always agree with what I know in my heart. There were so many things I did wrong, Iain. I should have stayed beside you, for one. Gran said that was why that woman, Lira," she said the name as if she'd just taken a mouthful of lemon slices, "it was why I found it so hard to resist…"

She broke off, guilt and shame washing over her at the memory. She was ashamed of how easily she'd been led, how easy it would have been to convince her to leave it all behind. She had come so close. She shot a furtive look over at Iain. His face, all chiseled Glencarragh good looks, was turned away from her, out over the horizon. She hadn't even told her gran that part. She couldn't bear to say the words aloud, instead, she buried the shame of it deeper into herself, determined to let it remind her of what it had cost them. She looked away from him, back across the sand towards the cliff, to the place where it had all happened, seemingly a lifetime ago.

Iain glanced over at her. She was still far too pale and thin. She admitted she was having difficulty sleeping, troubled as she was by the visions she'd seen on the night of the storm. Her bright red hair was a sharp contrast to the whiteness of her skin and her eyes were ringed with tiredness and sorrow. But there was a resolve in the set of her chin, and she walked straight and steadily.

"True enough," he said. "True enough. Although I don't know what good I would have been. The idea of me being able to stop you flying off into the wind seems a bit much, even for my superhuman talents."

In another time, his jests would have elicited a punch on the arm or a roll of her eyes. She simply smiled.

"Mrs.Glenbogie is going to help me," she said, "help *us*. She said we'll have to find others, before the next storm. Skelly told Gran something about there being other people who could help."

"Others?" he asked. "There are other wind-singers? I thought…"

"No," she said, "Seems I'm it for the wind-singing. Well, unless I have a daughter someday, I suppose."

Iain smiled at that, imagining the fortitude of any man who'd risk courting Cliona.

"No, Gran said there were other folk out there, two of them, to be precise who can help us. And Skelly isn't working alone, either. Supposedly, anyway. But who knows with that lot? It's all politics and pissing contests "

Cliona waved a hand towards the sea, a vague gesture of incomprehension.

"It's all annoyingly vague and I don't really understand it, to be honest."

She shrugged helplessly.

"The one thing she was quite clear on, unfortunately, is that without Skelly's help, we won't be able to manage *any* of it. We're equally beholden to one another, it seems. I don't know what Gran and Eileen were thinking of when they agreed to those terms. It's all very drastic."

Iain smiled a sad smile. He studied his friend's face as she frowned out at the rolling sea. She'd come a long way to understanding how much she belonged to the island, but he wasn't sure she was there yet.

"So, we keep holding up our end of the bargain, protecting

the selkies, or else Skelly won't help us," she continued. "He's got no sense of loyalty, you know."

Iain grinned at her indignation.

"No, I don't suppose he has. Feckless lot, aren't they?"

Cliona laughed.

"So how are you going to approach all this then? What happens next?"

Cliona sighed heavily.

"I've no idea, Iain. No idea at all."

# Chapter 22

"There you are!"

Iain grinned widely and enveloped Cliona in an encompassing hug.

Laughing, she shoved him away.

"Get off, you foolish creature. You've only been gone a couple of weeks. Don't get all soft on me."

"Aye, but I bet you missed me, didn't you?"

Cliona stuck out her tongue in answer and linked her arm in his.

"Let's walk down to the beach, shall we? You can catch me up on all that's going on in civilization."

Iain had been on the mainland doing a training course with the tourist charter company. They were expanding into bird-watching tours and needed more trained staff. It really had only been few weeks, but to Cliona, it felt like a lifetime. She glanced up at him as he chattered on about the pub nights and the hard slog of having to learn things from books that he'd rather learn as he went. Not to mention the hours spent on health and safety policies.

"It's all corporate mumbo jumbo," he said, finally. "I suppose they have to make us do it."

"Well of course they do," Cliona replied, sensibly. "What if some poor besotted mainlander forgets herself and veers too close to the railing, trying to get a closer glimpse of a lesser blue-tipped wag-wing, just as a gust of wind whips up? It would behoove the handsome captain to drop everything and dash to her assistance."

Iain gave her a sideways glance and saw the twinkle of mischief in her eyes. He gave her a friendly shove and the two burst into laughter.

"Leave off with that, will you? You'll never let me live that down."

"No, no I won't. I mean, it's not easy on the rest of us, basking in the glow of your celebrity."

She was referring to the way that women of a certain age seemed to gravitate towards Iain for photo opportunities. He seemed to exude the right combination of youth and ruggedness, combined with a genuinely friendly and helpful nature that made people want to be around him. Particularly women. The agent from the charter company knew exactly what he was doing when he'd signed Iain on.

"Aye, well, no. I suppose it isn't," he said, with mock severity. "Right, enough about me. How are you getting on? Your mam? How is she?"

"Oh, you know," said Cliona, with a smile of forced brightness. "It's up and down, as you'd expect."

"True enough," remarked Iain, studying her face. She'd walked a little way from him and was turned to look out over the sea, but he'd noticed the smudge of weariness under her eyes when she'd greeted him.

They walked in silence for a while, each lost in their own thoughts.

The sea ambled back and forth along the shore, unrecognizably gentle, after the raging might of the recent storm. The tang of salt and ozone prickled Cliona's nostrils and she found herself taking deep, steadying breaths, allowing the rhythm of the sea to soothe the anxiety that had followed her in the weeks since Ewan's and then, not long after, her gran's death. She may have appeared nonchalant to Iain, and most days she really did manage just fine, but there were moments when the deep, bleak, ache of loss stretched out before her like an impassable chasm, leaving her raw-throated and hollow. In addition, the weight of what her gran and Mrs.Glenbogie had told her lay heavily. It all seemed so impossible, like she was dealing with creatures and forces far beyond her experience, despite having been brought up with the lore of them. The story and the reality were very different beasts and without the quiet faith of her gran in her everydays, she wasn't sure she was up for it.

For his part, Iain was strangely content. The horror of having lost another fisherman, and one so very young, had sent the small community reeling. There was talk of phasing out fishing altogether, at least on a commercial scale. The popular point of discussion in the pub was that the storms were the faery folk exacting revenge for the area being over-fished. Iain had suppressed a wry smile at that, hiding his face behind his pint. They weren't far wrong in that. There was definitely faery revenge involved. In the end, it had all been bluster; the boats were still going out, but several of the older folk had announced they were selling up. The boats had been quickly snapped up by the tour company, who had been desperately wanting to expand the business but had been forestalled by some antiquated law governing boat traffic in the bay. As a result, the coming spring would see Iain as captain of his own boat.

"You'll be delighted with your new job, then?" said Cliona, breaking the silence. "Training courses notwithstanding, it's the perfect fit for you."

Iain's face creased into a happy grin.

"Aye, it is that. And yeah, I'm thrilled with it. I mean, I don't love that folk have given up their livelihood, but…"

"Don't be daft," said, Cliona, linking her arm into the crook of his elbow again. "Those old codgers were only putting in the time, anyway. Now they get to sit in the pub all day, spending the pots of money they got for their boats. Which, in other circumstances, would've been left on the beach to rot."

"True, I suppose," said Iain. "It was a clever thing for the company to do, though. To buy the rights to the original names. They can tout the history of the place now."

"Yes," said Cliona, lifting her other arm in a gesture miming that of a circus ringmaster.

"'Exploring the ancient lineage of Glencarragh, sail back in time on an historic fishing vessel…' Or some such touristy nonsense."

Iain threw his head back and laughed. His contentment and good fortune made it easy for him to see the silliness of it.

"Ah, but the punters love that sort of thing. Just like they love buying your 'authentic, hand-knit traditional island apparel…woven from an ancient lineage of native sheep'"

Cliona snorted.

"Touché," she said, smiling at the memory of the look on Dorothy McShane's face when Cliona had asked if she'd want to sell the various knitted garments she was commandeering from the local knitters group. She'd been reluctant at first, when it had been proposed that she become the official representative of the group, not believing she was in any position to organize such a thing. She was the younger member and had been erratic at best in her attendance over the years, disliking the implication of entrenching herself in something so traditionally Glencarragh. But since the loss of Ewan and her gran, she'd found a great deal of comfort in the warm kitchens and pleasant chatter of the women as they gathered to knit. She'd gratefully immersed herself in the community of women, accepting first their sympathy and then their encouragement as she'd been put forward as their spokesperson.

"It's an old medicine," Mrs.Glenbogie had explained, as they'd walked back together from such a session. Cliona had made a comment about the energy in the room, that particular day. Since the storm, she'd been irritatingly sensitive to certain energies. The women had been discussing the merits of a blend of herbs that could be used to treat a grandchild's rash. As the needles clacked, they resolved the best combination, the best place to find one of the ingredients and the easiest way to apply it. "There was a time when women on this island didn't have a lot of power over things. It was a way for them to wield their magic that wouldn't be so noticeable, aye?"

She'd given Cliona a sideways glance, curious to see how she would take the information. But Cliona had just kept walking, her face impassive.

"Penny for them?" said Iain, nudging her with his shoulder. "You're a million miles away."

Cliona looked up at her old friend. He'd aged a bit, since the storm. As had they all. There were tiny lines at the corner of his eyes that she hadn't noticed before, and dark smudges underneath them. But he was still Iain, still the one to see the bright side of everything. She resolved to try and be more like him in future.

"I was just thinking," she began, keeping her eyes forward, her gaze on the expanse of beach with its border of craggy cliff and temperamental sea.

"About?" prodded Iain.

"About maybe looking into setting up a wee dress shop. Eventually, I mean. After a while. Nothing too grand, just something to keep my hand in with clothing design, you know?"

"Oh?" Iain spoke with a held breath. He didn't want her to see the delight on his face or hear it in his voice. Being too enthusiastic with Cliona had often backfired. "For the tourists, like?"

Cliona shook her head.

"Not necessarily. I was thinking more along the lines of repurposing old clothes into reproduction vintage designs and things like that," she flapped a hand, grinning at his look of confusion. "And, of course, making sure that Harpy McShane has a good supply of linen aprons and knitted vests and whatever else the punters want."

Iain nodded. That he could understand.

"And something else," continued Cliona, with slightly less confidence. "I thought maybe I'd go in for a course in herbalism or something like that. I mean, I can learn from the women here, they probably know more than any class, but I was thinking I'd need a certificate. You know, so that I could have some official credibility. I would need that, you see, if I wanted to sell things. You know, lotions and teas and such…"

Her voice trailed away as her confidence faltered. It was the first time she'd spoken the idea aloud. And it wasn't something she'd ever given serious thought, it just sort of crept up on her one day as she'd sat staring out across the moors. It felt like something more to connect her to her gran and the long line of island women from which she was descended.

Iain took a deep breath and stopped walking. With her arm linked in his, Cliona had no choice but to also stop. He looked into the face of his childhood friend, seeing the familiar fire that always flickered below the surface. Only now, it was a dampened under something else. Fear, perhaps? A closely guarded vulnerability? Or perhaps it was simply the weight of grief and all that had happened in the previous weeks. Whatever it was, it had changed her. It had changed them all.

"You'll be staying, then?" he asked, gently and with caution, knowing any discussion of Cliona's future plans was a mine-field.

Cliona turned her face away from his, looking out towards the distant horizon.

She sighed and turned back to him, smiling.

"It looks like it," she said, extracting her arm from his and smoothing down her hair, which had been plucked from its scarf by a ripple of the rising wind. "You know, I thought that this whole wind-singer legacy foolishness meant I didn't have a choice anymore. It certainly seemed that way, having it shoved on me like it was. But if there's one thing I've learned since that bloody horrible day up on the cliff, is that choices aren't always so black and white, you know?"

Iain didn't speak. He let her pause in silence, knowing how difficult it was for her to say the things she was saying. He studied her profile, seeing the set of her jaw and the muscles of her face working hard to stay calm. Her hair had escaped again and was flying in a wild halo around her head as the wind danced in from the sea.

"Sometimes there's more to it than staying or going," she continued. "And sometimes, letting one thing go, means you get to hold something else, something you didn't even know you wanted, a whole lot closer."

She swallowed hard, turning back to face him, her eyes bright. Iain felt his heart break just a little.

"Besides," she said, punching him hard on the arm. "There's work to do and I can't very well leave you bumbling lot to do it, can I?"

She fumbled in her coat pocket and pulled out a crumpled rectangle of paper.

"Which reminds me," she said, tugging his sleeve. "There's something I have to do."

Iain watched her walk down to the edge of the water and pause, recognizing with only a small twinge of unease, the posture of the wind singer.

Her hair streamed behind her as the wind swirled and eddied, dancing to a gentle summoning. She wanted to be sure the envelope didn't come back.

Crouching down, she placed the well-read letter on the surface of the water, watching as the ink of the Paris postmark bled and faded. The tide reached out foamy fingers and plucked it from Cliona's grasp, tugging it along as it retreated back from the land and toward the depths of the sea.

Just as she rose to stand, a glint of something green caught her eye as the sea pulled back the sand on its retreat. Laughing softly to herself, she reached and picked up the piece of worn glass, closing her hand over the tingle of magic. An exchange, then.

# Epilogue

The bell tinkled merrily as she pushed open the door of the shop. The inside was crammed full of everything from traditional crafts to cheap tat, the over-riding theme being one of separating the tourists from their money. Dorothy McShane was nothing if not a shrewd judge of the eager droves who craved a piece of the strange island and quaint fishing village to take home.

Cliona sighed.

In the months after the storm, with Ewan gone and her father drifting listlessly about, having no interest left in life at all, it had fallen to herself and her mother to bring in some extra money to keep them afloat. So, not only had she accepted the role as chief advocate of the knitting group, she was now also a great contributor to the wares they had for sale. In addition to the knits, she was slowly amassing a selection of linen garments, plant-dyed from the various leaves and berries that she foraged from the hedgerows. It gave her a strange sort of comfort to know that she was, in some way, making up for her failure to save Ewan from the storm. Because, despite reassurances to the contrary from everyone, that's exactly how she felt. She'd been selfish and arrogant, dismissive of the serious power she was wielding, and it had cost her brother his life. She would be paying for her mistakes for a long time to come.

"I'll be with you in just a moment!" called Dorothy's voice from the back room.

"It's just me, Mrs. McShane," answered Cliona. "No need to rush!"

"Aye, righto then. I'm just boiling the kettle, lass."

Realizing she wasn't a well-heeled customer, Dorothy lapsed back into her usual accent. She could put it on or off and even thicken it, depending on who she thought she was dealing with.

Cliona set down the basket of knitted hats and socks.

"Genuine native wool — gathered from the sheep that dot the very moors around us. 'Tis spun by the hands of fisher wives and knit into the traditional patterns that have been handed down among the women of fishing communities for hundreds of years".

That was the spin that Dorothy put on the items that Cliona and her knitting ladies made. They sold like hotcakes, especially in the early spring and autumn when the winds of Glencarragh were particularly inhospitable to the tourists. Cliona had offered to knit some jumpers of her own designs as well, but Dorothy had dissuaded her.

"Not yet, pet. Not 'til they're absolutely desperate for them. They'll no' blink at the price tag for a jumper once they've spent a good while in the warm embrace of those socks."

Cliona wandered around the shop, touching the piles of rough, beige, roving and smoothing her hands over the carved, wooden figures of seals. Smiling inwardly, she wondered if any of the tourists really believed in the selkies of Glencarragh, or if they were just happy to go along with the copy of the holiday brochures.

*If only they knew*, she mused.

Turning the corner at the end of the aisle, she came to a wall hung with paintings. There were the usual seascapes and portraits of the bright fishing boats tied up in the harbor, but there was a small collection in the corner that caught her eye.

With a swift intake of breath, she reached out and picked up the largest of the paintings.

"Strange bit isn't it?" said Dorothy's voice behind her. "I'm not sure what got into me on the day I said I'd take them on. They're not the usual style for the shop, aye?" she waved a heavily ringed hand around the display of standard fishing-village artwork.

Cliona traced a finger across the paint. The colors of the sea seemed to move and shift and the sky rolled with storm clouds. But it was the figures rendered in the grey-black sky that had grabbed her attention.

Clearing her throat, she said, quite casually.

"Yes, it's very odd. But there's something quite appealing,"

Dorothy grunted.

"Aye, well. There's no accounting for taste. The punters seem to like them, anyhow."

"Is it...are they done by a local artist, then?" Cliona asked, putting the painting down with trembling hands. "I thought I knew everyone who painted around here."

"Och, no! Tis a new lass, come last month or so from the mainland. She's living up at one of the old crofting cottages on the north moor. A queer artist type, you know the sort. Bit stand-offish if you ask me. Right, what've you got for me today? I'm almost out of the socks...."

* * *

Cliona huffed and puffed her way to the crest of the moor. It was a particularly blustery day and her headscarf flapped violently, threatening to tear itself loose and run off with the wind. The cottage was just visible among a stand of thorny wild roses. A spray of honeysuckle clung desperately to the tumbledown wall that surrounded the tiny white building. A spiral of smoke curled from the single chimney.

"Oh good," thought Cliona. "At least there's someone home after this trek."

Suddenly a shape burst from the hedge. A flash of white and brown hurtled toward her and she stepped back in surprise, catching her foot on a tuft of heather and falling down with a thump, spilling the contents of the basket she'd had hung over her arm.

"Angus! Angus!" cried a voice. "Bloody hell, dog! What've you done now?"

Cliona felt her arm being tugged and she struggled to stand.

A fair-haired woman, of about her own age, looked worriedly on. Her attacker, a small, boisterous terrier by the looks of it, ran around in excited circles with the packet of chocolate biscuits from her basket in his mouth.

"I'm terribly sorry," said the woman, dusting invisible dirt from Cliona's coat. "He's not usually quite so…. well, yes, he is. I'm so very sorry! We don't get many visitors up here and I think he's forgotten how to act in polite society. Erm, can I offer you a cup of tea, as restitution?"

Cliona smiled.

"Yes, thank you. That would be lovely. I'm Cliona, by the way," she said, holding out her hand.

The woman smiled back, a warm grin that lit up her face. She wiped her hand down her paint-splattered jeans and shook

Cliona's.

"Nice to meet you, Cliona. I'm Frances." The little dog ran up to Cliona and dropped the biscuits at her feet. The packet was crushed and dripping with slobber.

The two women looked at each other and laughed.

"And this is Angus."

The End

# About the Author

Melanie Leavey was born and raised in the north-east of England before emigrating to Canada with her family at the age of nine. An aspiring hermit and passionate gardener, she likes nothing better than drinking tea and thumbing through the pages of the latest David Austin rose catalogue. A country mouse turned town mouse, she lives with her husband, two children, a badly-behaved Jack Russell and a cat named George in Fort Erie, Ontario.

Learn more and stay up to date with new releases by visiting her website and/or signing up for her newsletter.

**You can connect with me on:**

🌐 https://www.threeravens.ca

🔗 https://www.instagram.com/melanie.leavey.writes

**Subscribe to my newsletter:**

✉ https://tinyurl.com/ufgrrqh

CPSIA information can be obtained
at www.ICGtesting.com
Printed in the USA
BVHW071331210720
584140BV00002B/17